The Renewed Earth

STANDING IN HOLY PLACES

BOOK FIVE

THE RENEWED EARTH

BY CHAD DAYBELL

spring creek
BOOK COMPANY
Provo, Utah

ISBN 13: 978-1-932898-63-7
e. 1

Published by:
Spring Creek Book Company
P.O. Box 50355
Provo, Utah 84605-0355

www.springcreekbooks.com

Cover design © Spring Creek Book Company
Cover image © Raycan | Dreamstime.com

Printed in the United States of America
Printed on acid-free paper

AUTHOR'S NOTE

As I complete the final volume in this series, it has been interesting to look back at what has happened nationally and globally since the release in 2007 of the series' first volume, *The Great Gathering*. Prophesied events seem to be falling into place at a more rapid rate. China and Russia continue to strengthen their militaries, while the social unrest beginning in Tunisia and spreading to Egypt and Libya signals a change in the Middle East and throughout the world.

Meanwhile, the massive amount of government debt in the United States is causing distress in many states and raising deep concern on a national level. The time to prepare does seem to be growing short.

As you conclude this series, I would recommend you read the book *Through the Window of Life* by Suzanne Freeman, a dear friend of mine who had a near-death experience in 1999. During her time in the Spirit World, the Savior showed her several upcoming world events which parallel much of this series' storyline. Suzanne is a faithful Latter-day Saint, and although you gain a sense of her beliefs throughout the book, she purposely wrote it so it would be accessible to all Christian readers.

There are a few differences in our portrayals of future events, which should be expected, since my series is fiction and her account is not. I would highly recommend her book if you have enjoyed this series. It will ring true to you, and I think you will particularly enjoy Suzanne's account of the return of the Ten Tribes.

I want to thank all of the editors who have helped me so much with the process of writing this series, but particularly my father Jack Daybell, Galen Fletcher, and Jarom Huff. These three men don't really even know each other, but their varying backgrounds have been extremely helpful to me right from the beginning of the series, and they each provided dozens of suggestions and ideas that strengthened the books.

I want to thank my wife Tammy once again for her constant love and support, and I also thank my children Garth, Emma, Seth, Leah, and Mark for their insights on the series. They are all wonderful people, and I'm proud of each of them.

Finally, I thank all of the readers who have been so supportive. Your emails and positive comments have meant the world to me, and I'm grateful to you for spreading the word about the series to your family and friends. I hope you'll be satisfied with the conclusion!

Chad Daybell
March 2011

THE FINAL MOMENTS

Four months have passed since the historic meeting at Adam-ondi-Ahman the previous fall. As the calendar turns to January and another year begins, a strange winter season has gripped the earth. There is a constant chill in the air, and there has hardly been any precipitation across the earth. No one can really remember when the last good rainstorm took place.

Despite the prolonged famine, the Saints throughout the Americas are prospering, thanks to an abundance of natural springs that have emerged within their Cities of Light. The Saints have gratefully acknowledged the hand of the Lord in watching over them.

Four of the seven plagues in the Book of Revelation have been fulfilled. The fourth plague's prolonged intense heat was so devastating that it reduced the earth's population by nearly a billion people, particularly in the Coalition countries.

The Saints are anxiously awaiting the next plague, which they know from the scriptures will also impact the entire world through some form of pain and darkness. The prophet has told the Saints he isn't sure how it will come to pass, but to prepare themselves by continuing to stock each home with plenty of food and water.

Meanwhile, Elias has become the undisputed leader of the Coalition nations. As Gog, the head of Magog, he has taken on a god-like, almost mythical status among the people of Europe and Asia. Millions of people in Islamic nations consider him to be the Twelfth Imam that has come to destroy the infidels, while Christians are convinced he is the Antichrist prophesied of in the

1

Bible. Elias rarely makes public appearances, but his image and speeches are broadcast via satellite regularly to all of the Coalition cities, with entire nations willing to obey his commands.

Elias is currently following Satan's command to organize a massive Coalition army in order to crush the two apostles in Jerusalem who have protected the city for more than three years as the Jews hurry to complete their temple where the Dome of the Rock once stood.

The three main couples in this series continue to make valuable contributions to the Lord's kingdom. As this volume begins:

Tad and Emma North live in New Jerusalem with their children Charles and Leah. The Norths' son David resides with his wife Phyllis and their two-year-old daughter Kiffon in a student housing complex near the BYU-Zion campus. Both David and Phyllis are close to earning their degrees.

Tad is still the bishop in their ward located a few miles from the New Jerusalem Temple, while Emma continues to serve as their ward's Relief Society president.

Tad and Emma still often talk about what they experienced during the meeting at Adam-ondi-Ahman the previous fall, and they know the Second Coming is very near.

Doug and Becky Dalton now live in Springville, Utah, where Doug has served in several capacities in helping rebuild the city. Doug still retains his calling as one of the 144,000 high priests called to seek out faithful Saints and gather them to Zion, and he expects to depart soon on yet another mission.

Becky is now teaching elementary school in the Grant School building, where their children Heather and Justin attend.

The Daltons' young son Daniel passed away the previous year, but they received great comfort when Kim Brown told them of her experience in the Spirit World where she saw Daniel teaching the gospel to their ancestors.

Josh and Kim Brown have now been apart for more than three years while he carries out his duties as an apostle in Israel, and their hearts never really stop aching for each other.

However, it has been a great blessing for Kim to continue living among the Guatemalan Saints in Zion, whom she considers to be a wonderful extended family. She continues to serve as a Family History online data coordinator for the Church. She has been able to devote more time to that assignment now that the Browns' twins, Timothy and Tina, have turned five years old and are attending school. They are curious, bright children who barely remember their father, but Kim has told them all about him and promises them they'll see him soon.

Now on with the story.

CHAPTER I

John the Revelator stood silently on a small rock outcropping in southern Iceland, surrounded by flowing streams of molten lava. Less than a mile away the island's volcano known as Katla rumbled for several seconds before sending another blast of lava and ash into the sky, obscuring the noontime sun.

"Magnificent!" John said to himself. He had witnessed many amazing acts of nature during his 2,000 years on earth, but few scenes matched the fury of a volcano at full-throttle.

John had actually first seen this volcano in a vision in 96 A.D. on the Isle of Patmos while he was writing the Book of Revelation. The scene had impressed him then, and he had vowed to somehow view the actual event in person when the moment arrived. Now he was within seconds of the big finale.

Another strong tremor shook the ground, and John nearly tumbled into the lava, but he straightened himself and smiled as the volcano belched forth a tremendous burst of ash.

"That should do it," John said, remembering the scene from his earlier vision. He instinctively crouched down and braced himself.

BOOM!

In an instant the volcano exploded like a fiery torch, sending enormous amounts of debris into the sky, and creating a toxic black cloud that quickly covered the area.

The explosion tossed John violently through the air before submerging him in a torrent of water that was pouring from a rapidly melting glacier nearby. He surfaced and wiped the water from his eyes. The volcano was now steadily spewing thick black ash, which was being caught by the wind and drifting eastward. John knew the ash cloud would fill the skies over Europe within hours and then eventually encircle the globe, causing worldwide distress and chaos.

"The fifth plague has finally begun," John said.

At that moment, Elders Josh Brown and Colton Negus stood in the Court of the Priests on the Temple Mount in Jerusalem, gazing up with admiration at the nearly completed Jewish temple.

"I can't imagine that any of the previous temples built here looked any better than this one does," Colton said.

"Hey, don't get too boastful," Josh responded, giving his fellow apostle a grin. "You're right, though."

This edifice was actually the fourth temple the Jews had built on Mount Moriah in the past 3,000 years. The first was built by King Solomon around 950 B.C., and later destroyed by the Babylonians in 586 B.C.

The second temple on the site was completed in 515 B.C. Centuries later—around 20 A.D.—the temple was completely renovated by Herod the Great and was known as Herod's Temple during Jesus Christ's mortal ministry. That temple was destroyed by the Romans in 70 A.D. during their siege of Jerusalem, and from that time until the 21st century, the only identifiable remnant of the temple was a portion known as the West Wall.

However, a splendid temple now towered on Mount Moriah once again. As the temple's construction had progressed, thousands of Jews had made their way to Israel from throughout Europe and Asia, miraculously eluding the Coalition's border patrols. They brought with them their treasures and riches, which had been used to decorate the temple. When the apostles would ask these new arrivals why they had made such a dangerous journey, they would simply say, "We were aware of the perils of traveling here, but the urge within us was so strong we had no choice."

✢ ✢ ✢

Josh's thoughts about the previous temples were interrupted when he felt a swoosh of the air next to him. John the Revelator was now standing at his side, sopping wet and coated with what looked like black tar. Josh gave John a bewildered look and asked, "Where have you been?"

John looked down at himself and shook his head. "Sorry for the mess, but I've just been in Iceland—or what's left of it. The Katla volcano has exploded, taking part of the entire island with it. The resulting ash cloud will create the fifth plague. It happened just as I saw it in vision many centuries ago."

Colton turned to look at John. "Did you say this explosion is tied to the fifth plague?"

John nodded then quoted his own writings from Revelation 16:10-11:

"And the fifth angel poured out his vial upon the seat of the beast; and his kingdom was full of darkness; and they gnawed their tongues for pain,

"And blasphemed the God of heaven because of their pains and their sores; and repented not of their deeds."

Colton raised his eyebrows. "So the fifth plague is volcanic ash?"

"Yes, that's the main trigger of the upcoming destruction," John said. "The ash will affect millions of people across the world, but the bulk of the cloud is headed straight toward 'the seat of the beast,' meaning Russia. It will also directly hit the Coalition army that Elias is leading here."

"Do you know where Elias is right now?" Josh asked.

"They've passed through Turkey and will soon reach northern Syria, but the ash cloud will stop them for a time."

"How will the plague affect us here in Jerusalem?" Josh asked. "Is there anything we can do to protect the people?"

John frowned briefly, as if seeing in his mind once again the troubles that lay ahead. "Israel is right in the ash's path, but you can certainly use your priesthood power to divert it. Do everything you can to make sure the temple is dedicated as scheduled."

"We will," Josh said, looking at Colton. "We need to talk with Benjamin Cohen and let him know what's coming so he can alert the people about how to prepare."

"Very good," John said. "I'm going to go get cleaned up, but let me know if you need anything in the next few days."

John then vanished, and the apostles began walking briskly toward Benjamin's home to inform him of the plague.

CHAPTER 2

⸙

That same evening, Elias walked alone across a hill in northern Syria, delighted by the sight of millions of Coalition soldiers setting up their tents in the valley below. This massive group was on its way to his hometown of Damascus, where Elias planned to coordinate a series of overwhelming ground assaults on the cities of Israel, culminating with the conquest of Jerusalem.

He was certain such a wave of attacks would be too much for the two apostles to handle. If all went well, they would be killed and all of the Jews living in Israel annihilated.

Elias was ready to return to his waiting guards at the bottom of the hill when he felt a presence materialize next to him.

"Hello, Master," Elias said, glancing at Satan and then back at the throngs of soldiers. "They're quite an impressive sight, aren't they?"

"They'll be unstoppable," Satan said, truly pleased at the size of the army. "You've done well. Israel will soon be ours."

The unexpected praise from Satan allowed Elias to momentarily forget the military failures he'd experienced lately. After initially promising Satan he would assemble a massive army within a month, Elias changed his mind and tried to frighten the Israelis with several air attacks in hopes of scaring the Jews into surrendering without a fight. However, the apostles had used their priesthood power to make a mockery of Elias' efforts. He had fired the artillery at all times of day and night, but none of the Coalition's missiles or aircraft had even reached Jerusalem.

"Don't those two ever sleep?" Elias had shouted after yet another failure. Elias didn't realize the apostles had been warned by John the Revelator of Elias' plans, so they had adjusted their sleeping schedules so that at least one of them was awake at all times.

Elias' most frustrating day had been when he'd sent a squadron of Coalition aircraft to bomb the outskirts of Jerusalem, but in response the apostles created intense downdrafts directly in the planes' path. The wind and the planes met right above the Sea of Galilee, and within seconds there were dozens of expensive planes plunging into the water.

In frustration, Elias had immediately ordered several high-powered missiles to be fired at Israel, but as these weapons approached Jerusalem, their electronic components short-circuited. Even worse for Elias, the missiles somehow turned in the sky back to their point of origin, which resulted in the destruction of several Coalition missile launchers.

After that disastrous day, Satan appeared again to Elias and threw a ten-minute temper tantrum because he hadn't followed their original plan.

"Are you stupid?" Satan had shouted in Elias' face. "You'll never overcome the apostles through modern technology."

Elias had meekly bowed his head and said, "I thought it might be a quick way to solve the problem."

"No, the real problem is that you still underestimate them," Satan responded in a slightly calmer voice. "They have the power to command the elements, and that seems to include electronic devices. Our plan to overwhelm them with sheer manpower is the only way to stop them. There will be just too many soldiers for them to keep track of."

Elias finally saw the logic of Satan's point of view. "Don't worry, I've learned my lesson. We'll do as you outlined, and once those two are dead, the Jews will either bow down to our army or face extermination."

So Elias went to work on their original plan. He had told Satan he would soon have 200 million men ready to crush Israel, and they actually met that goal by recruiting all males over age 14 throughout Europe and Asia—with the promise of steady pay with plenty of food and housing for their families.

The soldiers had gathered on the outskirts of Moscow and began their march toward Israel in late January. The worldwide famine made the wintertime journey much easier without snowstorms to contend with, but the trek through southern Russia's Caucasus Mountains—situated between the Black Sea and the Caspian Sea—had taken much longer than anyone had anticipated. The rugged mountain passes had worn out the soldiers, but after they emerged from the mountains and spent a few days along the Tigris River, the soldiers were feeling refreshed and morale was high.

The Coalition army had since moved halfway between the Tigris and Euphrates rivers, and Elias had noted the symbolism as the army passed through Mesopotamia, the so-called "Cradle of Civilization." Scientists felt this area had been the location of some of earth's earliest civilizations, so Elias felt it was fitting he was leading an army through this same area.

"Enjoy this historic scenery," he told his generals. "You'll always remember this journey as the final step in establishing the greatest civilization of all time."

A few hours after the Iceland eruption, Elias was jolted awake around midnight by an urgent phone message from Moscow. A Coalition scientist reported to him that a monstrous explosion had destroyed part of Iceland and a dense ash cloud was already making its way across Europe.

"Does it look like we'll be okay?" he asked.

"No. The cloud is so vast it will hit Moscow hard, as well as the Middle East."

"How does it compare to previous eruptions?" Elias asked. "I don't want to overreact about it."

"I assure you this is much worse than anything we've ever seen," the scientist replied. "I truly fear it will make breathing difficult for anyone in the cloud's path, and it could even lead to respiratory failure in many people. I would get your soldiers somewhere safe as soon as possible."

Elias abruptly ended the conversation and rushed outside his tent to look at the sky. The stars were visible directly above him, but something was definitely blocking the stars on the western horizon.

Elias cursed under his breath. He was tired of these obstacles that kept emerging. He shook his head in disbelief that an Icelandic volcano was once again affecting his life.

The first time had been when he was a college student at Columbia University in New York City in the spring of 2010. His freshman year had been challenging and frustrating as he adjusted to the frantic pace of American life. He felt invisible and unimportant. He yearned to return to his life in Syria, where he had received special treatment.

As Elias finished his final exams that spring, he impulsively purchased an airline ticket to return home. Then came the volcanic eruption in Iceland that shut down overseas travel to more than 20 countries for several days. During that period of waiting, Elias spent a lot of time wandering through Central Park, often sitting quietly under a tree for several hours. It dawned on him that if he returned to Syria, the kind benefactor who had paid for his college would consider his efforts wasted.

That is when Elias carefully evaluated his life and eventually decided to stay in the United States. He took the money from his airline ticket refund and bought a large tent that he erected in Central Park near the spot where he had meditated. He began inviting park visitors into his tent to discuss a variety of topics and quickly gained a large following.

Soon his life was propelled in a new direction when New York City officials ordered him to remove his tent from the park. To the officials' surprise, thousands of Elias' supporters jammed the park for several days and rallied to his defense. The story made national headlines, and the city officials finally let Elias keep his tent there, leading to his unusual celebrity status. The marvelous events that soon followed in his life never would have happened if that Icelandic volcano hadn't erupted and he had boarded that airplane home to Syria.

So naturally Elias had always felt the Icelandic ash was an omen of good fortune for him, but now it could turn into a catastrophe. The timing couldn't have been worse for the army, since they were currently a long distance away from a steady water supply. They had filled several water trucks to supply the troops until they reached another river, but because of the famine that still encompassed the earth, they would all be in trouble if they stayed in one place for too long.

Elias pondered for a moment, then realized his best bet was to march the army to the Euphrates River several miles to the west, where they would at least have adequate water and hopefully find better shelter than their tents. Elias had his guards awaken all of his generals, and after they gathered in his tent he explained the situation to them.

"Let's get the tents down and everything packed," Elias said. "I want to be marching within the hour. Our scientists made it clear this is very serious."

As the generals scattered, Elias stepped outside and checked the sky again. The cloud was advancing rapidly toward them.

"Step it up," Elias shouted at two lingering generals. "We don't have time to waste!"

✣ ✣ ✣

As Elias had requested, the Coalition army was moving west within an hour, but it was much more difficult to maneuver such a large group in the dark. In fact, this was the first time they had ever traveled at night, and as the caravan of soldiers crawled at a snail's pace, tempers flared among the soldiers. They didn't fully understand why they had been ordered to pack up and move almost immediately after getting their tents set up. But as midnight approached, ash began to silently descend on the Coalition army.

"Hey, it's snowing," one soldier called out.

"No, you idiot, it's volcanic ash," his general responded. "That's why we need to keep moving."

At first the soldiers didn't seem affected, but as the night wore on, nearly everyone was coughing and their eyes were itching.

Dawn arrived, but very little sunlight reached the troops—just enough that they could see three inches of ash now covered the ground, blanketing the entire landscape and nearly blending in with the gray sky. It was a nightmarish scene that provoked howls of frustration and anger from the soldiers. The ash continued to steadily fall from the sky, growing deeper by the hour.

During the formation of the army, Elias had bonded with an experienced Egyptian general named Hisham Ramez, and he trusted his judgment completely. However, on the trek to the Euphrates River, General Ramez was in the final group of soldiers making sure no stragglers were left behind. Feeling desperate for his advisor's guidance, Elias ordered, "Get on the radio and tell General Ramez to leave his position. I need him to join me at the front of the army immediately!"

Meanwhile, a cleaned-up John the Revelator had transported himself inside the New Jerusalem Temple. He knew the members of the First Presidency were holding a special evening meeting to discuss the reports coming from the satellite about the volcano, and he needed to share with them the events taking place in Europe and the Middle East.

John paused briefly outside the door to their meeting room and gave a unique knock he had worked out with the prophet. Within seconds the door opened, and he was welcomed into the room.

"I'm sorry to interrupt," John said to the leaders, "but the events in Jerusalem are accelerating."

The prophet motioned for John to join him at the head of the table. "We're glad to see you," he said. "The satellite broadcast that we were able to intercept from Europe is talking about a huge ash cloud. We're wondering if it is tied to the fifth plague."

"Yes. The ash is from an Icelandic volcano that has erupted, and the cloud is heading directly over Europe and Asia. The ash is also causing trouble for the Coalition army that is currently marching toward Jerusalem. Within days the ash will circle the planet and affect the Cities of Zion as well."

"How are the apostles in Jerusalem doing?" the prophet asked. "Have they been affected by this?"

"They will be," John said, "but I'm confident they'll find a way to make this situation work out for the best."

The prophet looked thoughtfully at John. "The time is nearly here, though, correct?"

"Yes," John said somberly. "It has been almost three and a half years since our brethren arrived in Jerusalem. The prophecies will surely be fulfilled."

The prophet nodded. "John, we want to hear more from you on how we can prepare the Saints for this ash cloud, but first please join us as we kneel and pray for our fellow apostles."

"I would be honored," John said, joining the Lord's mortal leaders as they pleaded that Josh and Colton would receive the inspiration they needed to preserve Israel and the Jewish people.

CHAPTER 3

———— ❧ ————

At that moment, Josh and Colton stood at the window of their small home on Jerusalem's Temple Mount watching the volcanic ash settling on Jerusalem. The ash had been falling on the city for several hours, and a thick layer now coated the ground and covered the roof tops.

"It's coming down heavier than I thought it would," Josh said. "It's too late to divert it, but we need to put a stop to it somehow."

John had counseled them to keep the ash away from the city, but it had arrived during the night before they realized it. So as they had many times during their mission to Jerusalem, the apostles knelt down to pray. As each man pleaded to Heavenly Father for a solution to the situation, a phrase from Jeremiah 25:32 suddenly popped into Colton's mind: *"A great whirlwind shall be raised up from the coasts of the earth."*

"Hey, I think a hurricane would solve it," he said.

Josh glanced over at him thoughtfully. "Don't we need a large body of water for that?"

"Why couldn't we create one by using the Mediterranean Sea?" Colton asked. "Maybe the storm wouldn't be too powerful, but it would get the job done."

Josh nodded, picturing it in his mind. "If we brought it toward Jerusalem slowly, the hurricane's outer wall would blow away the ash that has covered the city. Then we could position the eye of the hurricane over Jerusalem, which would hopefully protect us from receiving more ash."

"Sounds good to me," Colton said, and the apostles knelt down briefly once again, thanking Heavenly Father for providing the inspiration for their plan. Then they hurriedly dressed and walked through the ash-covered streets to Benjamin Cohen's house. They wanted him to warn everyone of the need for the city's inhabitants to be indoors for the next few hours until the hurricane's eye was above the city.

When the apostles arrived at Benjamin's house, they were greeted by Benjamin's niece Rachel Cohen, a slim dark-haired woman in her late twenties with vibrant eyes and a quick smile.

"It's good to see you both again," Rachel said as the apostles stomped the ash from their shoes on the porch.

Her uncle Benjamin joined them and added, "Isn't this ash a nightmare? I'm surprised you're both not coughing after walking so far in it."

"We're all right," Josh said, holding up the cloth he had been breathing through during their walk. "Don't worry, we're going to take care of the ash."

"How?" Rachel asked. "This seems like a monstrous task, even for you."

Colton gave her a small grin. "Don't forget that with God nothing is impossible, especially with hurricane-force winds on your side."

Rachel's eyes widened. "You're going to create a hurricane?"

"That's the plan," Colton responded. "If we create it over the Mediterranean Sea, the storm's winds will hopefully blow the ash out of Jerusalem. Then we'll move the eye of the storm over the city, giving us clear weather, but at the same time keeping the Coalition army at bay."

"That really sounds like it will work," Benjamin said. "When can you get started?"

"We're ready when you're ready," Colton said. "How long will it take to spread the word for everyone to stay indoors for the next while?"

"Less than an hour," Benjamin said. "We'll get right on it."

✤ ✤ ✤

When the apostles first met Rachel two weeks earlier, the Spirit strongly testified to them that she would play a key role in the events leading to the Savior's upcoming appearance in Jerusalem. However, as they had first chatted with her, she was somewhat cold toward them, giving curt, short answers.

Soon afterward, the apostles met again with Benjamin, and Josh asked him, "Could you please tell us about Rachel? We both feel she has the potential to be a great leader among your people—even though she doesn't seem to like us."

Benjamin smiled. "She's a feisty one who is very cautious in everything she does. She's endured much suffering in her life, and that's mainly why she acts so standoffish. She can be quite vocal at times, though, and if she's on your side, she'll defend you to the end."

"She told us she was attending a university in Greece," Colton said. "How did she end up there?"

"It was partly to just get away from here after her parents' fatal car crash three years ago," Benjamin replied. "My brother Joseph and his wife were wonderful people, and when they died it really devastated Rachel."

"So I'm guessing she grew up here in Israel?" Josh asked.

"Yes, she served for two years in the IDF—the Israel Defense Forces—and rose quickly up the ranks. She was strongly considering a military career until her parents' deaths, and that's when she decided to go to Greece."

"Well, maybe she'll warm up to us eventually."

"I think she will," Benjamin said. "I agree with you that she has returned here for a special reason. Even until just a few weeks ago, she would call me from the university and tell me how much she enjoyed Greece. She had no intention of ever coming back to Jerusalem. So I was very surprised when she appeared on my doorstep last month and asked if she could stay with me. I actually urged her to go back to Greece because of the threat from the Coalition army, but she explained she had suddenly felt an overwhelming yearning to return to Israel."

"That's interesting," Josh said. "It seems to be happening a lot lately among your people."

"More than you know," Benjamin said. "I know of thousands of Jews who have expressed those same feelings in recent years, especially after we started rebuilding the temple. It's as if God is calling them home to the land of their forefathers. So they come, ready to face whatever awaits them."

Rachel's coldness toward the apostles had softened considerably since their first meeting. She had initially been very wary of her uncle's devotion to these two men, and she was certain they were only there to take advantage of her people in some way.

However, a few days after her arrival she was walking along the street and noticed Elder Negus talking to a crowd of people. He took a small crippled girl in his arms and blessed the child to walk through the power of God. To Rachel's amazement, the bones in the girl's legs straightened out, and when the apostle placed her down on the ground, she immediately took several steps to her mother.

Everyone in the crowd rejoiced, and Rachel knew she had witnessed a miracle. She had stayed nearby—but out of his sight—as he performed several other healings in the following hour. She then ran to Benjamin's home and told him what she had seen.

"The healings appeared completely real," she said. "I know he didn't see me, so I'm sure it wasn't some sort of act in my behalf. But what if we're somehow being deceived?"

"I had the same feelings when they first arrived, but I realized there are only two options," Benjamin said. "Either these men are of God, or they are frauds. I have come to the conclusion they have been sent by God to help save our people. I believe you'll come to feel the same way."

"So you trust them?" she asked.

"Absolutely," he responded. "Don't forget that I've been misled before. I was certain that Elias was here to help us. Instead, he's using the information I gave him to try to destroy us. I promise you I would never have trusted these apostles if God hadn't given me an assurance they are telling the truth."

That conversation came back to Rachel as she raced through the streets of Jerusalem to warn the citizens about the upcoming hurricane. She stopped in her tracks as it powerfully struck her heart that the apostles truly were there to help her people.

"Dear God, thank you for sending the apostles to us," she prayed. "Please help them protect us!"

As Rachel and Benjamin spread the word throughout the city, the apostles went to Benjamin's second-story balcony and gazed at the unending ash cloud. After praying together for the Lord's blessing on their efforts, Josh reached out in the direction of the Mediterranean Sea and commanded the elements to produce a small hurricane.

They waited for nearly five minutes, but then they could faintly see through the ash some towering thunderclouds beginning to form on the western horizon. Soon the distant clouds had developed into a massive wall, and lightning occasionally flashed through the sky.

Colton put his hand on Josh's shoulder. "I'd say the storm is developing as planned."

Josh nodded. "We'll let it ferment for a while until we hear from Benjamin and Rachel."

As if on cue, they noticed Rachel running in the street below them and then heard her slam the front door. She ran up the stairs and entered the patio.

"Whew, I'm out of breath," she said. "But I noticed some clouds starting to form!"

"Yes, it looks like the storm is underway," Colton said. "How is it going among the people?"

"Very well," she replied. "We've made sure someone in each neighborhood has been notified, and they'll contact each house."

"Then it sounds like we can proceed," Josh said. "I'm going to move the storm toward the city."

Following Josh's commands, the storm rapidly progressed toward Jerusalem, and soon large gusts of wind began blowing the ash out of the streets just as Benjamin arrived home. The winds continued to accelerate, and finally they all moved back into the house and shut the patio door.

"Aren't you afraid the wind is going to break everyone's windows?" Rachel asked.

"We're okay," Josh reassured her. "The eye of the storm will be over us in just a few minutes. Besides, the winds right now are probably only in the range of a small tropical storm. Once we have the eye positioned above the city, we'll increase the storm's intensity and see if we can give the Coalition army enough wind to make them buckle down for a while."

Later that afternoon, Elias was sitting huddled inside a jeep that was rocking back and forth from the strong winds. He had spent the past hour trying to reach the Coalition's top meteorologist, Ivan Medved, via a satellite phone hookup. Ivan's sole job was making sure he warned Elias of any approaching storms so the Coalition army could adequately prepare, but Ivan hadn't contacted him about this one.

The sky darkened and heavy drops of rain began to pelt the windshield. Finally the scientist was on the line, and Elias unleashed his anger.

"Why wasn't I warned about this storm?" Elias demanded. "I have the entire army out in the open!"

"I'm terribly sorry, but there wasn't even a storm system in the area this morning," Ivan said. "I've never seen anything like it."

"What do you mean?" Elias asked.

"The storm emerged from nowhere over the Mediterranean Sea

only a few hours ago, but now it's already a monstrous Category 4 hurricane. You're being hit by the outer edges."

Elias pictured in his mind the region's geography. "So where is the eye of the storm?" he asked, already sensing the answer.

"The city of Jerusalem," Ivan responded.

Elias gritted his teeth, then let out a string of profanities. "It's those apostles again! They must be destroyed!"

As the night wore on the storm got increasingly intense, tipping over some of the vehicles and making it impossible to keep their tents in place. The soldiers had no choice but to lay inside the collapsed tents to try to stay dry. No one could sleep as the hurricane continued to pound them.

General Ramez arrived during the night, having traveled against his best judgment in the treacherous conditions, but he knew Elias could make some poor military decisions when he was angry. He found Elias still in his jeep and climbed inside with him as the wind nearly blew the door off the vehicle. Ramez struggled to shut the door, but it finally latched. He then calmly turned to Elias and said, "I'm here, sir. Let's discuss our options."

Elias was so relieved to see his leading general that he almost broke into tears. "I'm so glad you made it. We need to wipe Jerusalem's inhabitants from the face of the earth immediately. I don't care how many men we lose."

"Calm down," Ramez said soothingly. "We're still in control. This storm can't last forever, and when it stops, we'll march the soldiers to the Euphrates River, where we can regroup and finalize our assault on Jerusalem."

Elias took some deep breaths, knowing he was starting to think irrationally. "You're right. That's why I need you by my side."

"I'm not going anywhere," Ramez said. "I want those Jews dead just as much as you do."

The apostles allowed the storm to remain over Jerusalem for another full day, but it began to naturally weaken. So rather than prolong the storm, they commanded it to move to the northeast and pass directly over the Coalition army, giving the soldiers one final drenching.

Once the storm dissipated, the Coalition army did move forward to the Euphrates River, which was now surging beyond its banks due to the storm. The water was even above some of the bridges. It would be a few days before they could cross the river, but no one minded. They were more concerned about drying out all of their equipment.

Despite their problems, the Coalition soldiers were much better off than if they were still in Moscow. The ash cloud had completely encompassed the northern latitudes, and all of Russia was hit very hard. Sunlight barely filtered through, and millions of citizens died painfully that first day from severe respiratory problems. Additional millions died within days because of a lack of drinkable water, truly fulfilling the Bible's prophecy of the fifth plague by "bringing darkness upon the beast's place."

CHAPTER 4

Tad and Emma North stood outside the Thomas S. Monson Events Center on the BYU-Zion campus with their son David and his little daughter Kiffon. They had just attended the graduation ceremony for their daughter-in-law Phyllis.

After Kiffon's birth, Phyllis had diligently taken online classes and completed her bachelor's degree in U.S. History with an emphasis on the period between 2001 and the collapse of the U.S. government. Her intent was to become a history teacher once the Millennium began.

Emma played with Kiffon along a small stream as they waited, and soon Phyllis emerged from the building. They gave her a cheer and plenty of hugs.

"Congratulations," Tad said. "You're going to be a fantastic teacher."

"Thank you," she responded. "I couldn't have done it without all of your support."

"I'm so proud of you," David told her. "Now I need to get my degree finished up too."

Emma gave Phyllis another hug. "Yes, keep pushing him along. We're going to need astronomers in the Millennium as well."

As they were standing there, a man called out, "The prophet has announced that the fifth plague has begun in Europe and Asia."

The crowd gasped, unsure what to do. "Do you have more information?" Tad said, noting that the man was reading the message from a handheld device.

"Apparently a volcano in Iceland has blown up and the ash will

24

reach us soon," the man said. "The prophet said we need to return to our homes and he'll speak to us over the Internet at 1 p.m."

Several hours later Emma and Tad rested quietly in their bed after a long day of canvassing the ward with other ward leaders. They had made sure each family was fully equipped with medical masks to filter out the ash if needed, as well as plenty of food and water. They had also discussed with their children Charles and Leah during dinner about how to prepare for the coming plague.

The prophet had said in his message that Europe and Asia were already receiving the brunt of the plague and that millions had died. He emphasized that he didn't expect the ash to be as thick by the time it circled the earth and reached North America, but that the Saints would certainly be affected soon.

As Emma lay in bed, she pondered the onset of another plague and realized there were few prophecies left to fulfill before the Second Coming. She raised up on one elbow and asked, "Where does the City of Enoch fit into all of this? Shouldn't it have returned by now?"

Tad chuckled and turned to his bed stand, where he switched on the lamp and grabbed his scriptures. "I'm not quite sure. Let's see what the Lord says about it."

He turned to The Pearl of Great Price and started reading Moses 7:60:

"And the Lord said unto Enoch: As I live, even so will I come in the last days, in the days of wickedness and vengeance, to fulfil the oath which I have made unto you concerning the children of Noah;

"And the day shall come that the earth shall rest, but before that day the heavens shall be darkened, and a veil of darkness shall cover the earth; and the heavens shall shake, and also the earth; and great tribulations shall be among the children of men, but my people will I preserve."

Tad paused and said, "That certainly sounds like what we've lived through lately."

"I'd say," Emma agreed. "I'm ready for these plagues to be finished."

"I'll continue reading," Tad said. *"And righteousness will I send down out of heaven; and truth will I send forth out of the earth, to bear testimony of mine Only Begotten; his resurrection from the dead; yea, and also the resurrection of all men; and righteousness and truth will I cause to sweep the earth as with a flood, to gather out mine elect from the four quarters of the earth, unto a place which I shall prepare, an Holy City, that my people may gird up their loins, and be looking forth for the time of my coming; for there shall be my tabernacle, and it shall be called Zion, a New Jerusalem."*

Tad chuckled. "I can actually remember reading that verse while I was on my mission and telling my companion that the building of Zion would never happen in my lifetime, but now I *live* in New Jerusalem!"

"I think my brother Doug's service with the 144,000 certainly qualifies as gathering the elect and sending them to Zion," Emma added. "I feel that verse has been fulfilled. Keep reading."

"And the Lord said unto Enoch: Then shalt thou and all thy city meet them there, and we will receive them into our bosom, and they shall see us; and we will fall upon their necks, and they shall fall upon our necks, and we will kiss each other;

"And there shall be mine abode, and it shall be Zion, which shall come forth out of all the creations which I have made; and for the space of a thousand years the earth shall rest.

"And it came to pass that Enoch saw the day of the coming of the Son of Man, in the last days, to dwell on the earth in righteousness for the space of a thousand years."

Emma pondered for a moment. "That verse makes it sound like the City of Enoch won't return until after the start of the Millennium."

"I believe you're right," Tad said, before skipping down the page to verse 69. "I really like this verse that describes the city's inhabitants when it was taken into heaven. I hope those of us in New Jerusalem can measure up to their standard."

Tad then read, *"And Enoch and all his people walked with God, and he dwelt in the midst of Zion; and it came to pass that Zion was not, for God received it up into his own bosom; and from thence went forth the saying, Zion is fled."*

Suddenly Emma's chest began to burn, and she started to weep. Tad put his hand on her cheek and asked, "What's wrong?"

"Oh, nothing's wrong," she said, "but when you read that last verse, I just felt a strange connection to Enoch's people. It was as if the Spirit was testifying to me that they're our close friends, and we've really missed seeing each other."

Tad smiled at her. "I wouldn't doubt that at all."

CHAPTER 5

In another part of the Milky Way galaxy, a beautiful woman named Susannah was slowly walking through the rooms of the home where she had been raised. She gently touched treasured mementos that rested on the shelves and ran her fingers along the door frames.

"I've missed this place," she said to herself.

It had been nearly 5,000 years since the Lord had translated the City of Enoch, removing the entire city and its inhabitants to the terrestrial realm of the galaxy. Since that time, Susannah and the city's other citizens had been serving in various capacities as translated beings on many planets throughout the Lord's kingdom, but they had all looked forward to the day when their city would return to its rightful place on earth. They were eager to join with their brothers and sisters in New Jerusalem.

Susannah was the first member of her family to arrive back home, and she thought that was fitting. As the oldest child in the family, she would be there to welcome the other siblings back. Of course, her younger brother Enoch likely was too busy to stop by the house, but she expected to see him later that day at the meeting that had been scheduled outside the main temple.

She settled into a chair and let her mind wander back in time. As a translated being, Susannah had been granted the privilege of remembering her premortal life, and her dearest friend there had been a splendid woman who had been born on earth as Emma Dalton. Susannah and Emma had known each other for eons of time, and they had always been united in their faith in Heavenly

Father's plan. They had vigorously defended the Plan of Happiness during the War in Heaven, and they had comforted each other when Lucifer led away so many of their spirit siblings.

After the War in Heaven, Heavenly Father's most valiant spirit children were separated and prepared to live during crucial times on the earth that was being created for them. As they sat together in a heavenly flower garden, their angel tutors explained that there would be a 6,000-year period between when Adam and Eve would leave the Garden of Eden and when the Savior would return to begin the Millennium.

The angels explained that the Savior himself would live on the earth at about the 4,000-year mark during a time of great wickedness.

"I want to live then and defend him," Emma had said, but the angels told them that it was necessary for the Savior to be killed in order to complete the Atonement and redeem the world.

"Then I want to go when I am most needed," she replied.

The angels smiled at her determination. One of the angels told them, "There will be two vital times when the Lord will most need his faithful Saints to stand strong against wickedness. The first era will take place just a few hundred years after Adam and Eve have passed away. Despite their valiant efforts, most of their descendants will become wicked and turn from the truth. However, there will be a family line of righteous children who will be true to the gospel despite great opposition, and they'll eventually create the first Zion society."

"I like the sound of that," Susannah said. "But tell us about the other time."

"The second era will take place toward the end of the earth's history," the angel said. "This will be just prior to the Savior's Second Coming. It will also be a time of great wickedness, but the righteous Saints of that day will build a city called New Jerusalem and create a Zion society to help usher in the Millennium."

"It's a difficult choice," Susannah said. "However, I feel that I should live during that first era. I want to be an example that creating Zion on earth is possible, so that later generations will have our city to aspire to."

"That sounds good," Emma said. "I'll join you there. Maybe we can be sisters!"

Heavenly Father had allowed these valiant children to have a say in the organization of their earthly families, and it was soon approved for Susannah and Emma to indeed be sisters on earth. Even more exciting was that their little brother would be Enoch, who had been foreordained to create the Zion society.

However, as the hours passed after the decision was made, Emma felt unsettled. This wasn't a common feeling for her in the premortal world, and she sensed the reason behind it. She had developed a strong bond with a man who would later be known on earth as Tad North, and he had already committed to help build the Zion society planned for the latter days. Tad had even asked Emma to join him there and be his eternal companion.

Emma was worried she had hastily made a wrong decision, and she finally decided to talk to her eldest brother Jesus about it. She found him at one of the temples and told him of her inner struggles.

"Yes, let's talk about it, but please bring Tad with you," Jesus said. "I'll meet you at the temple gates."

"Thank you so much," Emma told him before rushing to find Tad.

Soon the three of them were walking together through a beautiful garden. Emma quickly explained the situation to Tad, who hadn't yet heard about Emma's decision to be Susannah's sister.

"I don't like this at all," Tad told her. "I thought we had an understanding!"

"I know," she said anxiously. She turned to Jesus and pleaded, "Help me!"

Jesus smiled and put his arms around each of them. "Emma, I know you want to live when Susannah does, but Heavenly Father and I need strong leaders to build New Jerusalem. Tad will be one of them. Please consider living in the last days, where you two can marry and raise righteous children. You will influence many people for good and live to see my Second Coming."

Jesus then explained more about the assignments they would receive on earth, and while Emma was sad she'd be separated from Susannah, she could see the wonderful life she and Tad could experience together.

"I'll do it," she finally said, clutching Tad's hand. "I'll join you in the latter days."

"That is a wise choice," Jesus said. "You'll be greatly blessed, and I know Susannah will understand."

Emma's decision came as a surprise to Susannah, but she readily accepted the change in plans, knowing it was for the best. When the time came for Susannah to be sent to earth, the two friends had hugged each other tightly and shed some tears.

Susannah could hardly believe the time had nearly arrived when they would be able to embrace each other once again.

Later that day, most of Susannah's siblings and their families had gathered at their home as they returned from their various assignments throughout the galaxy. Soon the group began walking together toward the temple.

"Aunt Susannah, where's Uncle Helam?" one of her nephews asked.

"He's already at the temple," she responded about her husband. "Your Uncle Enoch asked him to help prepare for the meeting."

"Helam always was one of Enoch's favorites," another sister teased.

"Well, he's one of my favorites, too," Susannah responded with a smile.

Susannah looked around at her family members—all descendants of the original patriarchal line. Her father Jared was the fifth generation from Adam and Eve through the lineage of their son Seth. Her father was a righteous man who had raised his children to have faith in God during a very turbulent time when wickedness had prevailed in the earth.

When Susannah was a young girl, it had been understood that one of her brothers would be selected to continue the patriarchal line, and several of her brothers had definitely shown potential. In fact, the only brother who had been clearly ruled out as the next prophet was her younger brother Enoch. As a young man he had stuttered and stammered, and it had been hard sometimes to even understand him.

Susannah had taken Enoch under her wing and loved him as much—if not more—than her other siblings. He was often ridiculed by others because of his speech impediment and was essentially a social outcast. So she had been as shocked as anyone when Enoch came home one day completely cured of his ailment, saying the Lord had healed him and had called him to preach to the people.

Soon Enoch was preaching far and wide with great power, bringing many people to the gospel. The people he converted began working together to build a city, and Susannah and her parents moved there to join with them. She soon met Helam, and they were married in the new temple Enoch had built there.

However, Enoch's preaching had caused many other people to be stirred up against him, and a great army was formed to destroy Enoch and his people. At the precise moment the army was going to attack the city, Enoch called upon the powers of heaven and created a great earthquake, causing mountains to literally move into the army's path. The quake was so great that mighty rivers left their channels, and a new peninsula of land even formed in the sea.

This display of priesthood power was so memorable that their enemies never bothered Enoch or his people again, and the city flourished for more than 300 years before being taken into heaven by the Lord.

✤ ✤ ✤

As the group reached the temple, Susannah saw Enoch standing on the stairway leading to the temple's main door, greeting many family members and friends. He spotted her and motioned her forward.

"It's wonderful to see you again," he said, giving her an embrace and a peck on the cheek. "Helam said the two of you have been very busy."

"We've done our best with our assignments," she replied, "but I'm eager to return to earth. I'm excited to see my friend Emma again. It has been too long."

"Well, once we settle down next to New Jerusalem you can seek her out," Enoch said. "She might not remember you at first, but the Holy Ghost will open her mind to many pleasant memories. You know, she desired long ago to live with you on earth. That righteous desire will soon be fulfilled, although not in the way she expected. You'll both be living in the New Jerusalem together when the time is right."

"That's what I'm counting on," Susannah said.

Helam was motioning for her to join him in the crowd below, so she gave Enoch another quick hug then moved toward her husband. Enoch climbed to the top of the stairway so he could see the entire group that had gathered.

"Welcome, my beloved brothers and sisters," Enoch shouted. "What a glorious day!"

He then spent several minutes explaining the details of what lay ahead for them. He concluded the meeting by saying, "Soon we will set foot again on the earth we cherish, where we will receive resurrected celestial bodies and live in happiness with our Savior. Blessed be the name of the Lord."

The crowd cheered, eagerly anticipating that great event.

Chapter 6

Back on earth, Doug Dalton was slowly driving his solar-powered truck along a crumbling and broken Interstate 80 in northern California. The sky was very hazy as the first clouds of ash from the Icelandic volcano were reaching North America. The ash was lightly coating everything, and he had to use his windshield wipers occasionally to keep the glass clean.

He and Jonas Ferguson were on their way to check on the temples in the region. In the past month, the First Presidency had fully organized the 144,000 high priests who would scour the earth to seek out anyone who would accept the gospel before the Second Coming of Jesus Christ.

Doug had already been serving in the calling as a member of the tribe of Ephraim, but now 12,000 men from each tribe had been called and sent forth into the world one last time. Since Doug was already in Utah, he had been assigned to go to the West Coast. Most of the cities with temples throughout North America had already been rebuilt as Cities of Light, but due to the mass destruction along the coastline from both the Coalition invasion and several natural disasters, this part of the continent hadn't been repopulated with Saints.

A member of the 144,000 had already visited California the previous year without much success, but the General Authorities had felt prompted to send Doug there again, sensing that other members of the Church had gathered together since that time and needed to be informed about the Cities of Light that had been built by the Saints.

The First Presidency encouraged the 144,000 to choose a fellow Melchizedek Priesthood holder to serve as a companion. Doug had immediately thought of Jonas, who was a convert to the Church and could share his story with the people they met.

Jonas and Doug had first headed directly to the temple in Vancouver, British Columbia, where a few dozen Saints had gathered. They instructed the people to travel to Rexburg, Idaho, the closest City of Light. The duo had then worked their way south to the numerous temples in Washington and Oregon, where they found additional people gathered on the temple grounds and sent them on their way.

Some of these people had been at the temples for several months and were barely surviving on meager scraps, but they felt they were being watched over. The people at some of the temples had experienced true miracles, with flocks of birds landing on the temple grounds and allowing themselves to be captured. The people were able to make their "bird stew" last a long time. Indeed, the Lord had not forgotten them.

As they traveled along I-80, Jonas' thoughts drifted to what he had left behind. When he had returned to Utah a few months earlier, he had felt inspired to organize an automobile recycling center like the one where he had worked in New Jerusalem. After discussing the idea with Doug and other Church leaders, he had located the center in west Springville with the hope of giving the boys who had lived in Lincoln Point a meaningful purpose.

Jonas had asked Mighty Tom to be his right-hand man at the recycling center, and Tom's magnetic personality had drawn in those boys who had decided to keep living in Lincoln Point. Now they were all working hard, and they absolutely loved collecting the old vehicles off the streets and tearing them apart.

With Tom's help, Jonas organized a two-acre area with several dismantling stations so several cars could be worked on at once. The railroad lines between Utah and New Jerusalem had recently been restored, so Jonas made sure the final station was right next to the tracks so they could ship the recycled parts back to the larger plant in New Jerusalem.

They had teams of boys retrieving abandoned cars from as far north as Lehi and as far south as Santaquin in a never-ending cycle. Jonas was working ten hours a day to keep things rolling, and he was loving every minute of it. He felt pleased they were beautifying the cities and recycling the vehicles—while saving the boys' souls in the process. So Doug's request for him to be his missionary traveling companion came as a surprise, but he felt confident Tom would be able to handle the operation.

"You're a natural leader," Jonas had told Tom. "I'm confident everything will run smoothly."

"Don't worry, I'll keep the boys in line," Tom had replied, and Jonas was sure he was keeping his word.

As Doug and Jonas visited the temples, they discovered that very few of the people gathered there were non-members. The vast number of these people had been inactive Mormons at the time of the Coalition invasion and hadn't even been aware of the prophet's invitation to gather to the mountain refuges. These people had suffered greatly over the past few years for not being prepared to heed the prophet's voice at that time, but later on the Holy Ghost had prompted them to go to the closest temple, where Doug and Jonas were now able to tell them how to reach the nearest City of Light.

After checking the Sacramento Temple and finding no one there, they were now heading west toward the Oakland Temple. Doug knew the San Francisco Bay area had already been heavily damaged by a series of earthquakes and tsunamis, but he wasn't prepared for the devastation as they finally reached San Francisco itself.

As they traveled along I-80 near Berkeley, they could look across the bay and see that all of the key bridges had been ripped apart.

Far to the west they could see only see one of the Golden Gate Bridge's towers still standing upright. The other one was jutting out of the water at a strange angle.

The hillsides around the San Francisco Bay looked like they had been tipped sideways, causing the homes and businesses to stack up against each other like dominos.

"Wow, this is really frightening," Doug said. "When I was a teenager my parents brought Emma and I here on a vacation. The streets were crammed with cars and people, and it was filled with exotic sights and sounds. We drove up and down those steep hills and even took a family photo on the shoreline over there. Now there's nothing but silence. I can hardly believe this."

Jonas turned away from the window as he realized what he thought were piles of seaweed along the shore were actually decaying human bodies. "Oh, this is horrifying," he said. "I wonder if there will even be anyone at the temple."

"Well, we need to check for sure, even if it seems unlikely," Doug replied. "Show me the way."

Jonas pulled out their map and directed Doug through the ghostly remnants of the city of Oakland and up a hillside to the temple. The road was so bad that Doug had to shift the truck into four-wheel drive and maneuver one tire at a time over some of the cracks in the pavement.

An hour later Doug finally pulled the truck into the Oakland Temple parking lot, and the men could see a few people milling around near the front of the building. They all stopped and stared at the truck, then they started to panic and scatter. Doug and Jonas were used to such a response, and they hurriedly parked the truck and hopped out.

"We're members of the LDS Church and we're here to help you," Doug called out.

Three of the men looked at each other, then approached Doug cautiously. "Did you say you're members of the Church?" one of them asked.

"Yes, we have great news," Doug said. "The Saints have built marvelous cities in the Rocky Mountains, and we invite you to join them there."

After a few more questions, the men felt sure Doug was telling the truth, and soon the entire group of about 100 people had emerged from their hiding places.

"I think this is the biggest group we've seen yet," Jonas said to Doug. "I'm glad we didn't skip them."

As the people gathered around, Doug explained to the people in great detail about the Cities of Light, and it made everyone quite excited to know a flourishing civilization of Saints still existed.

"They have running water and electricity?" a man asked. "I can hardly remember a city like that!"

"Don't worry, you'll be there soon," Doug said. "I'll contact the leaders in Salt Lake City, and they'll send buses to take you to Utah. We just came down I-80 though, and with all of the freeway damage I doubt the buses can get closer than Sacramento. So over the next couple of days, gather everything you want to take with you and then begin walking there."

Doug and Jonas stayed with the Saints until they were ready to travel as a group. During the preparations, they spoke with each person and gave priesthood blessings to several of them who were sick or injured. Only one man in the group held the Melchizedek Priesthood, and he hadn't felt worthy to give blessings, so the people eagerly accepted blessings from the newcomers.

Jonas appreciated that the Lord had remembered these Saints as the Second Coming approached. These people hadn't heeded the prophet's warnings a few years earlier, but now they had been humbled and were eager to do the Lord's will.

Jonas enjoyed hearing the individual stories of how they had each found their way to the temple. One older black woman said she had been living in Oakland when a voice told her to drop everything and hurry to the temple.

"I was baptized when I was young, but I hadn't been back to Church in years," she said. "That voice was pretty demanding, though, and an hour after I got here, the first big quake struck."

"From what I can tell, the earthquakes have been pretty rough," Jonas said.

"That first one was unbelievable," she said. "I was outside here on the grounds, and I literally was bouncing off the grass. I don't know what the quake's magnitude was, but it was at least a 9.5 on the Richter scale. I swear the temple itself hopped a foot or two into the air."

"That's crazy," Jonas said with a laugh. "Have the quakes been happening often?"

"The big ones have hit every few days until lately," she said. "I suppose you're our good luck charm."

"Maybe so. I know the Lord is watching over us as we travel to each of the temples."

The woman smiled at him. "Thank you for finding us. We were starting to get desperate." She paused and wiped away a tear before adding, "You two remind me of the parable in the Bible where the shepherd searches for the lost sheep, even though he still has the ninety and nine back at his home. We surely qualify as a bunch of lost sheep."

"Oh, I wouldn't say that," Jonas said. "I'm impressed how you've bonded together and survived."

As Jonas moved away from the woman to help a young boy pack some clothes in a bag, a sense of joy filled his heart. He quietly gave thanks that he had been an instrument in opening a way for these good people to rejoin the Lord's flock.

CHAPTER 7

Over in Jerusalem, a top Israeli military general was meeting with the apostles and Benjamin Cohen in an office near the temple site. The Israelis had sent spies into Syria to monitor the activities of the Coalition forces, and the general had just received a final update for the day.

"The combination of the ash and the hurricane has greatly weakened their men," the general reported. "Nearly every soldier is suffering in some way, and there have been many deaths. However, Elias is forcing them to move ahead. It appears they'll stay camped on the Euphrates River until morning before launching a full-scale attack on Jerusalem."

"How many soldiers do you estimate they still have?" Benjamin asked.

"They've lost a few million men over the past week, but they also just received reinforcements from Iran," the general said. "That puts them back to nearly 200 million soldiers."

The group went silent. The number of men at the Coalition's disposal was truly frightening. They could easily swarm over Israel like locusts, leaving nothing behind.

Benjamin turned to the apostles. "We had planned to wait on dedicating the temple until next week, but I feel we need to move it up, possibly even tomorrow. How do you feel about it?"

Josh nodded. "There are only a few minor details left to finish the temple interior, and we could have a crew work through the night to complete them. Let's plan on tomorrow."

Colton spoke up. "But what if the Coalition really does launch

40

their ground attack within the next day? They could reach us within hours. That would really put a damper on the ceremony."

"Then we need to stall them somehow," Benjamin said. "It's essential we have the temple dedicated."

"I've got an idea," Josh said, turning to the general. "Do you have a detailed map of where the Coalition is camped? I particularly want the coordinates of the Euphrates River north of the camp."

"I can have them for you shortly," the general responded.

"That will do," Josh said. "We'll be waiting."

Josh motioned for Colton to join him in a side room, and he explained what he had in mind. Colton nodded and whispered, "The sixth plague. *'And the sixth angel poured out his vial upon the great river Euphrates; and the water thereof was dried up.'*"

"Exactly," Josh said. "We are that angel. It's in our hands now. I feel if we trigger the plague right after sunset, it will have the greatest effect."

"I agree," Colton said, looking out the window at the sinking sun. "Once we get those maps, let's not hesitate."

Within fifteen minutes, the apostles were carefully studying a detailed topographical map of northern Syria. Josh double-checked the latitude and longitude lines before using a red pen to pinpoint a certain location on the map. It was now dark outside, and Josh said, "I think we can proceed."

Josh and Colton held the map between them and knelt down. The others in the room instinctively joined them on their knees, then Josh prayed, "Heavenly Father, we desperately need thy aid once again. This will be a new approach to accomplishing a miracle, but through the Melchizedek Priesthood I hold, I command the ground located at the precise location I marked on this map to convulse and rip apart, causing the Euphrates River to disappear into the earth. I do this in the name of Jesus Christ, Amen."

After a horrible week, Elias was finally feeling in control of the army again as darkness settled over the Coalition camp. The ash that had tormented them had finally dissipated, and although the storm had left them beaten down and frustrated, they were ready to move forward. In the morning they would cross over the Euphrates River and begin their quest to conquer Jerusalem.

Before settling down for the night, Elias decided to take a walk throughout the camp to check on the soldiers' morale. Accompanied by two guards with flashlights, he moved toward the river's edge, where several tents were occupied by his top military leaders. As they approached the tent, a faint sound of thunder reached them.

One of the guards grabbed his arm and said, "Sir, did you hear that thunder? I hope another storm isn't coming."

Elias shook his head. "Did you say thunder? That sounded more like a rumble to me."

Suddenly he and the guards were jolted off their feet as the ground shifted nearly five yards to the east. Large cracks formed in the ground around them and a chorus of frightened shouts filled the air from the nearby tents.

Elias was briefly stunned, but he quickly got to his feet. He had experienced earthquakes before, but never one so powerful. He looked toward the tents along the river, and they were being knocked down by a wall of water. The earthquake had caused the river to actually slosh back and forth.

Elias spent the next hour making sure the troops were okay. He was grateful there had only been a few lives lost in the earthquake. He had expected some aftershocks, but the ground had been quiet since the initial jolt. He was definitely wary of unusual events by now and he was always looking for ways to blame the apostles in Jerusalem, but this one appeared to simply be a natural occurrence. He finally settled into his bed around midnight, but he slept fitfully. Something didn't feel right to him.

Elias was abruptly awakened at dawn by one of his guards.

"Sir, please come outside," the guard said. "We have a big problem on our hands."

As he left his tent, Elias gazed toward the river and was left speechless. The area where a mighty river had flowed the night before was now a 400-yard-wide stretch of dark mud. He turned to look at the bridge they had planned to cross that morning and saw two sections had collapsed, making it unusable.

"How is this possible?" Elias asked in dismay. "Where has the river gone?"

He hurried down to the leadership tent and found his top military advisors huddled around a radio listening to an incoming transmission. When they saw Elias walk in, General Hisham Ramez hurried to his side. Over the past few months, the former Egyptian revolutionary leader had emerged as Elias' key advisor. He was a large gruff man with graying hair and a ghastly scar that ran down the right side of his face. No one could remember seeing him smile.

Ramez had been a member of the Egyptian Army in early 2011 when his countrymen created an uprising and ousted President Mubarak. He had been in Cairo's Tahrir Square during those chaotic days of protests, and he saw the upheaval as a chance to help spread his extremist beliefs throughout the world. As he participated in the successive uprisings that followed throughout the Middle East, he gained greater notoriety and prominence.

When the Communists and Islamic extremists created a secret union based on their shared desire to overthrow America and conquer Israel, Ramez was right in the thick of the negotiations. As his stature continued to increase, he found himself in the inner circle of top military leaders that eventually became the Coalition's governing body. He had been chosen to personally lead the Coalition's attack against America, but shortly before his scheduled departure, an assassin attempted to kill him. Ramez was able to slay the assassin with his bare hands, but not before the attacker had sliced his face open, leaving the ugly scar he now carried.

The injury prevented Ramez from going to America, leaving him bitter and frustrated as he heard reports of the Coalition army's demise. He felt deep in his heart that the disastrous war effort in

America would have never happened if he had been in charge. He still couldn't understand why no one could give a straight answer on how they were defeated. For the time being, he was allowing Elias to satisfy his desire to conquer Israel, but Ramez still wanted another chance to subdue America.

Despite a major investigation, Ramez was never able to discover who had ordered the assassin's attack on him, which had left him paranoid and always questioning everyone's motives. But Ramez's surliness and distrust of others were partly why Elias had moved him into such a prominent position. Ramez had a fierce temper, and the Coalition soldiers feared and respected him. Elias knew Ramez's aggressive attitude was the perfect contrast to his own peaceful public image.

"Do we have any answers yet about what happened?" Elias asked Ramez.

"We do," Ramez said, pointing at the short-wave radio on a table. "We've just received word from our scouts that the earthquake opened a massive hole in the river bed about 15 miles north of here. The entire river is emptying into that hole and disappearing."

"What options do we have to cross the river?" Elias asked.

"Very few," Ramez responded. "The mud is impossible to cross, and every bridge between here and the hole has been severely damaged. Our only option is to travel north and get above the hole, where we can either find a usable bridge or start floating the soldiers across by boat."

Elias clutched the back of his neck in frustration. He had 200 million men ready to go to war, but they had been stopped by something as simple as mud.

"Then let's get moving north," he said. "We don't have any time to waste."

Ramez immediately took control, dispatching soldiers and relaying messages throughout the army's ranks. Elias was still slightly awed by Ramez's ability to effectively send instructions to their army of 200 million soldiers.

Later in the day a report came back that an intact bridge had been found 30 miles north of the army's campsite. It would be a major detour that would cost them a couple of days of travel time, but it was their only option to get to Jerusalem.

CHAPTER 8

While the Jewish leaders hurriedly prepared for the temple dedication, the apostles stayed with the Israeli military commanders, waiting for a report on the Coalition's response to the earthquake. Finally the word came that the army was moving north.

"That's great news," Josh said. "Let's get to the temple."

As the apostles walked across the city, Josh thought about the marvelous experiences he and Colton had witnessed as the time approached for the Savior to return again. During their time in Jerusalem, the apostles had purposely avoided teaching LDS doctrine to the Jewish people, but some of their miracles had been so overwhelming that many Jews demanded to know the source of their power. After receiving Benjamin's approval, the apostles began teaching a large group of people each night in the BYU Jerusalem Center.

These people were enthusiastic about the gospel, and after being taught the basic doctrines, they were baptized in the Jordan River, just as the Savior had been during his mortal life. These new Christian converts were thirsty for gospel knowledge, and there were now more than 500 members, organized into two wards.

These new Saints had wanted to live the Law of Consecration as the Saints were doing in the Cities of Light, and they begged the apostles to allow them to move into the building permanently, using the dormitories and even the classrooms to live in. It was a little tight on space, but the apostles could see the wisdom in such a move, and soon the long-vacant building was bustling with activity.

During the day, the Saints would go into the city among their Jewish brothers and sisters and perform acts of service. They didn't preach the gospel or share Christian messages, but instead sought to build friendships by emphasizing similar beliefs in God, and it had served them well. They were now beloved by their friends and neighbors for their kindness and charity.

The apostles would visit the two wards each Sunday and make sure everything was running smoothly, but otherwise they allowed the ward members to handle their own responsibilities. The apostles knew they had to keep their focus on their main role of protecting Jerusalem and preparing the Jews for the coming of the Messiah. The rebuilding of the temple had been a key part of this preparation, and the project had unified the people and strengthened their faith in God.

The apostles knew the true Messiah—Jesus Christ—would soon return, and then the Jews would understand that he had been their Messiah all along. They hoped all of the Jews in the city would be converted to the gospel of Jesus Christ at that time and receive the ordinances required for exaltation.

The apostles were eager to witness the pomp and pageantry of the temple dedication, which was already underway. They had been actively involved in the temple's construction, but they hadn't taken part in organizing the dedication services.

As the apostles approached the Temple Mount and entered the main court, they could see a choir on a stage singing a beautiful ancient ballad that shared the trials and triumphs of the Jewish people. Josh spotted their friend Rachel Cohen in the top row of the choir, singing her heart out.

Josh looked around for Benjamin, but he figured he was somewhere behind the scenes coordinating the ceremony and making sure everything was running smoothly.

The music was beautiful, and most of the thousands of people in attendance were openly weeping. These weren't tears of sorrow, however. Instead, their faces radiated sincere joy that the temple was at last being dedicated.

Colton scanned the area and marveled at what they had accomplished in such a short time since the destruction of the Dome of the Rock. The modern temple had many of the same features of Herod's temple, which had been destroyed almost 2,000 years before. Two large courtyards surrounded the temple itself, and an elaborate entrance to these courts had been built. As in Herod's day, this entryway was called "The Gate Beautiful."

Moving west from the courts to the temple, there were 15 steps leading up to the Court of the Priests. In this court was the altar of sacrifice and a multitude of drains to carry away the blood and water from the numerous sacrifices the Jews planned to perform after the Messiah returned.

From the Court of the Priests there were another 12 steps leading up the porch of the two-story temple itself, which was divided into the "Holy Place" and the "Holy of Holies." In the Holy Place was a large seven-branch menorah for light, a golden altar of incense for the daily prayer service, and a golden table for shew bread.

Two heavy veils hung from the ceiling within the temple. These veils separated the Holy Place from the Holy of Holies, a place reserved for direct communication with God. It had also been the sanctuary for the Ark of the Covenant, but this artifact had been lost when Jerusalem was destroyed in 587 B.C.

The precious metals and jewels that the Jews had brought to Jerusalem from across the world had been used extensively throughout the temple, including the front double-doors which were covered in gold.

It was indeed an impressive structure that stood as a testament of the resilience and perseverance of the Jewish people.

The dedication lasted for nearly two hours as the Jews celebrated this long-awaited event. Josh compared it to the elaborate pageants the Saints in Zion had often held prior to a dedication of their own temples. The dedication was filled with songs and performances intermingled with rabbis praising God. The apostles were particularly impressed by a group of men who each played a ram's horn, an instrument that had been blown on special occasions ever since the time of Moses when the House of Israel had departed from Egypt many centuries earlier. It was a fitting inclusion to the day's events.

As the festivities came to a close, Jerusalem's oldest rabbi took the stage and made a heartfelt plea to the heavens, asking God to accept this house and to find favor with the Jewish people for the sacrifice they had made in rebuilding it during a time of extreme hardship.

Colton was touched by the rabbi's words, and he knew the plea would soon be fulfilled when the Savior himself would visit the temple and accept it as a "House of the Lord."

Following the dedication, the apostles mingled with the crowds. A spirit of accomplishment and happiness filled the air, even with the knowledge that the Coalition army was planning to attack them within days. At this moment, everything seemed right with the world.

As the apostles prepared to return to the military command center to check on the Coalition's position, they were approached by their friend John the Revelator. They always found it humorous at how he just blended right in among the crowds.

"That was a very impressive ceremony," John said. "My people surely know how to celebrate, don't they?"

"That's true," Josh said. "These *are* your people."

"Yes. Sometimes the Saints forget that most of us who followed the Savior during his earthly ministry were Jews," John replied. "Speaking of that, I was hoping you could join me. There are several distinguished Jewish guests who were here to witness the dedication, and they would like to meet you."

"We would be honored," Josh said. "Where are they?"

"They aren't far," John said. "Follow me."

The apostles followed John through the streets, and soon they reached their destination—the Garden of Gethsemane on the western side of the Mount of Olives. The apostles raised their eyebrows at each other. Few modern-day Jews cared about this sacred garden, since they didn't believe in Jesus of Nazareth as their Savior.

"This seems like an unusual place for them to gather," Josh whispered to John. "I don't see anyone."

"Don't worry," John said. "They're on their way."

Suddenly three people appeared nearby, startling the apostles. A tall dark-haired man in a white robe stood beside a couple who appeared slightly older than him. They were also wearing white robes. The younger man stepped forward and extended his hand.

"Hello, my fellow servants," he said. "I am John the Baptist. I wanted to thank you for your service here in Jerusalem."

Josh's jaw dropped slightly, then he quickly shook John's hand with both of his. "The honor is mine," he said reverently.

Colton also shook John's hand before being introduced to John's parents, Zacharias and Elisabeth.

"Like John, we've also admired your valiant efforts here," Elisabeth told the apostles. "Without you, our people would have ceased to exist by now."

Colton wiped his eyes and hoped they didn't notice how hard his heart was pounding. "No, we need to thank you for devoting your lives to the cause of truth."

"We're grateful the Lord allowed us to be present on this day," Zacharias said. "This temple has special meaning to us."

Josh nodded reverently. It was in Herod's temple that Zacharias received an angelic visitation telling him that he and Elisabeth in their old age would have a son who would be the forbearer of the Son of God. It also was the place where he later was slain for refusing to tell Herod's soldiers where his infant son John was hidden.

John the Revelator motioned with his hand. "Josh and Colton, do you remember that my brother Andrew and I were disciples of John before we met Jesus? So this is a special reunion for me as well, because while John was a forerunner of the Savior's earthly ministry, you two are serving as forerunners of his millennial ministry."

The next few minutes were among the most enjoyable of Josh and Colton's lives as they conversed with these resurrected beings who had played such a vital role in the gospel plan.

Elisabeth made them laugh as she reminisced about the day Zacharias told her she was going to have a baby, and John smiled as he told them he never wanted to wear camel-hair clothing ever again.

"I'm sorry," Elisabeth told him with a smile. "We didn't have much else to work with in the desert!"

John grew more serious as he told of having to suffer for nearly a year in a damp, filthy prison for criticizing Herod's unlawful marriage to Herodias. Then came the awful decision by Herod to have John beheaded.

"But I have never regretted standing for righteousness," John said. "I have been blessed beyond measure."

Finally John the Revelator signaled that it was time for the apostles to return to the temple, and Josh and Colton had the privilege of receiving embraces from these wonderful people. They had always felt a surge of the Spirit when they visited with a translated being such as John the Revelator, but there was a much higher level of spiritual energy when a mortal touched a resurrected being.

Zacharias patted each apostle on the shoulder and said, "Stay strong, my dear brethren. Mortality is just a short moment."

"We will," Josh said, vowing to do the Lord's will at all costs, especially if it meant they could eternally enjoy the feelings of peace and security they felt while visiting with John the Baptist and his parents.

CHAPTER 9

Satan angrily watched the conclusion of the temple dedication from afar, just as he had during any major event involving the Jews or the Latter-day Saints. He was aware of the so-called "prophecies" made by Jesus' followers throughout the centuries, but he was convinced it was merely a failure on his part when one was actually fulfilled.

He knew his overall plan for world domination would work—he simply had to destroy all of the righteous people, either by killing them outright or by leading them away from Jesus' teachings. Once that task was completed, he would rule the earth.

After all, his plan had worked before. Less than two thousand years after Adam and Eve had left the Garden of Eden, he had successfully corrupted nearly all of their descendants. He felt only a global flood and a shipbuilder named Noah had stopped his carnal conquest of the human race, and he knew the odds of such a worldwide disaster ever happening again were astronomical.

However, it really upset Satan when his opposition actually fulfilled a major prophecy, coincidence or not. After the Roman army destroyed Herod's temple many centuries earlier, Satan had done everything in his power to make sure the Jews would never build another temple in Jerusalem. The construction of the Dome of the Rock had virtually assured that, but now standing before him was another Jewish temple on the Temple Mount. It made him burn with anger, and he placed the blame solely on the shoulders of one man—Elias of Syria. Within moments he was inside Elias' tent in the Syrian desert.

"You have failed me," Satan shouted at Elias. "The Jews dedicated their temple today in Jerusalem, and now they have even more spiritual power."

Elias was shocked that the Jews had completed the temple so quickly, but he also felt unjustly attacked by Satan.

"Do you realize what I've been through the past few days?" Elias shouted back. He knew it wasn't wise to yell at the devil himself, but he'd had enough bullying from him. "We've battled volcanic ash, a hurricane, and a major earthquake that blocked our way across the Euphrates River. Yet you expect us to still be on schedule to eliminate the Jews. What more do you want from me?"

Elias had said too much. Nothing infuriated Satan more than a leader who didn't show complete humility toward him. Satan leaped upon Elias like a crazed animal. Although he didn't have a mortal body, there were times when Satan was angry enough that he could literally crush the life out of a mortal who wasn't protected by Jesus' power.

"I can't breathe," Elias wheezed, feeling like his ribs were going to crack, but Satan simply tightened his grip.

"Is that all you have to say?"

"I'm sorry," Elias whispered. "You are the master, and I am the servant. I will do anything you ask."

Satan released his grip, and Elias lay gasping on the floor.

Satan stared at him for several seconds before saying, "You have one last chance to redeem yourself. If you aren't standing triumphantly in that Jewish temple in three days, I will replace you with someone who can actually complete this assignment. Any of your incompetent generals could have done the job by now."

The air stirred as the old serpent vanished from the tent, and Elias slowly crawled onto his bed for a brief recovery before assembling his generals to outline their new schedule. Soon he was on his feet. The rage he felt at both Satan and the apostles in Jerusalem who had thwarted him was enough to block out the agonizing pain caused by Satan's attack.

The Jews had basked in the glory of the temple dedication throughout the day, but by the next morning the seriousness of their situation became clear. An urgent message had arrived from the Israeli spies that the Coalition army was progressing across Syria at lightning speed. Some of the forces had already reached Damascus, putting them unnervingly close to Israel.

The Israeli leaders made a plea for every citizen with military experience to come forward and defend the nation. The response was overwhelming, since most Israelis had been drafted at age 18 to complete mandatory national military service.

Rachel Cohen had immediately joined the army, as had all of the Saints who were living at the BYU Jerusalem Center, except for a few mothers with small children. The Jewish Saints felt duty-bound to defend their country at all costs.

When the apostles learned that the Saints were going to battle, they understood their motivations. They visited the Saints before their departure and gave them blessings and encouragement. Josh spoke with Aaron Sondheim, one of the two bishops at the BYU building.

"You're making quite a sacrifice," Josh told him.

Bishop Sondheim shook his head. "This isn't a sacrifice for us, because we have an eternal perspective, thanks to you and Elder Negus. I was impressed with the story of Captain Moroni in the Book of Mormon, and how he rallied his people to defend their families and nation against their enemies. How could we not do the same?"

As the Israeli army began marching out of the north gates of Jerusalem, the apostles chose to spend the day there expressing their gratitude to these valiant men and women. Each soldier was dressed in military fatigues and carried a semi-automatic weapon with plenty of ammunition.

The apostles were impressed that although it had been several years since many of these soldiers had actively served in the military, they all were marching together in perfect rhythm. The soldiers' faces were filled with determination and few showed any fear of what awaited them.

The Jewish Saints soon marched past as a group, and they acknowledged the apostles with small waves and nods. Colton felt mixed emotions at seeing their cherished friends going to war. There was a real chance that nearly all of Jerusalem's LDS membership would be eliminated in one day.

"This could end badly," Colton said.

"I know, but I'm trying to keep an eternal perspective on it," Josh replied. "If they don't make it back, we know they'll go directly to Paradise and receive their eternal reward."

The apostles happened to spot Rachel coming toward them on the end of a row, which allowed her to briefly step out of marching formation to talk to them.

"I'll see you soon," Rachel said. "I know that God will be with us. Please watch over Uncle Benjamin."

"We will," Josh said.

"Send a miracle or two in our direction if you can," she added before hurrying back into formation.

Once the soldiers had left the city, the apostles returned again to the military command center to keep updated on the situation. The reports indicated the Coalition army was planning to move south from Damascus along the ancient road known as "The Way of the Sea." This route would lead the army past the Sea of Galilee and Mount Tabor before opening up into the Megiddo Valley, several miles north of Jerusalem.

After much discussion among the Israeli leaders, they decided to establish several lines of defense along the edges of the Megiddo Valley, while firing missiles and heavy artillery as the enemy soldiers first entered the valley. They hoped these tactics would buy them some time and keep the 200 million Coalition soldiers from entering the area all at once.

By the following morning, the Israeli army was nearly in place on the southern edge of the Megiddo Valley, but it was the speed of the Coalition army that astonished everyone. The first wave of enemy soldiers was already passing the Sea of Galilee, putting them within a few miles of the Israeli forces.

"I feel somewhat helpless," Josh told Colton. "I would love to cause a natural disaster right now to delay this, but I feel prompted by the Spirit that it's time for us to stand aside and let the prophecies be fulfilled."

Colton nodded sadly. "Besides, any miracles we perform to stop the Coalition army would likely end up killing some of our own soldiers as well. We've done all we can. Now we just have to watch how it all unfolds."

The apostles tried to remain positive about the outcome, but they understood scriptural prophecies as well as anyone. They were fully aware that the upcoming clash in the Megiddo Valley would soon go down in history by another name—the Battle of Armageddon.

CHAPTER 10

───── ⚜ ─────

Elias was watching his soldiers from the top of Mount Tabor at the northern end of the Megiddo Valley—a great, extended plain stretching from the Mediterranean Sea eastward across the northern part of Israel. The first Coalition troops were now funneling into the valley and were vulnerable to an Israeli attack.

"Come on, provoke us," Elias said to the Israeli military leaders who had assembled their forces on the southern side of the valley. "Do something to fire up my soldiers and let them know this isn't going to be a cakewalk."

As if on cue, a series of Israeli missiles flew through the air and exploded in the middle of the first group of Coalition troops. Several blackened craters were visible even from where he was, and his troops scattered in all directions.

"Finally," Elias said before walking to a nearby jeep where General Ramez was listening intently to reports from the front line.

"What was the damage from those missiles?" Elias asked.

"There were thousands of casualties," Ramez said. "Should we pull back until more of our soldiers have joined us?"

"Why would we do that?" Elias asked.

General Ramez gave his leader a sideways glance. In recent weeks, Elias had become completely desensitized to the value of human life, as if the soldiers were just pawns in a gigantic chess game.

"I'm just saying we might want to wait a couple of hours," Ramez said. "The narrow roads from Syria have funneled our troops into smaller groups and slowed us down. We have some soldiers that are still back at the Sea of Galilee and haven't even moved yet."

"We need to just plunge ahead," Elias said. "In fact, increase the speed of our march."

"But that is suicide for our soldiers if we —"

Elias glared at his general. "We have 200 million men at our command. Yes, we might lose a few million men at the beginning, but if we keep the pressure on, we'll eventually break through."

Ramez knew better than to argue with Elias, so he simply picked up his radio transmitter and contacted his leaders on the front line. "Gog has ordered that we continue the attack," he said. "Seek out any Israeli soldiers and destroy them."

"Excellent," Elias told him. "They can't stop us."

Despite Elias' boast, the Israeli army did indeed cause the Coalition forces to briefly grind to a halt as they unleashed a steady stream of missiles. But as Elias had hoped, the Coalition troops rallied against the opposition they faced. Thousands of Coalition soldiers were killed each minute, but many more than that were soon spreading out across the valley.

In Jerusalem's military command center, the Israeli leaders realized that hand-to-hand combat was inevitable. They told their generals to begin advancing across the valley toward the enemy.

Bishop Sondheim and the group of Saints were near the front lines, and as they saw the Coalition troops swarming toward them, terror briefly filled his heart. But then he turned to his group and shouted, "Let us set the example and show no fear! Get down and fire away!"

The Saints spread out in a line and lay flat on their stomachs, firing at the oncoming soldiers. They made a tremendous effort in slowing down the Coalition troops in front of them, killing hundreds of them within seconds. But the swarm just kept coming and firing back. Slowly the Saints were killed one by one.

After ten minutes of intense gunfire, Bishop Sondheim felt a sharp jolt in his neck. He reached up and saw blood covering his hand. A second bullet hit him in the chest, and his spirit left his body. As he slowly ascended into the air, he was greeted by a majestic angel who took him by the hand.

"Well done," the angel said.

Bishop Sondheim was confused. "Well done? I'm dead, and the Coalition is crushing us."

"Blessed is he who gives his life in defending righteousness," the angel responded. "You have earned your reward."

Bishop Sondheim then looked across the field and saw thousands of angels hovering above the Israeli army. When soldiers were killed, angels immediately swooped down and greeted them.

Then he looked to the north and only saw a few angels above the Coalition troops, although he saw millions of dark spirits mingling among the soldiers.

"Their dead soldiers aren't going to the same place you are," the angel said.

"But I see a few angels over there," the bishop said.

"Yes, there are a few good souls who really had no choice in joining their army," the angels said. "But most of them aren't going anywhere."

"What do you mean?"

"Watch."

Bishop Sondheim then saw a Coalition soldier get killed, but when his body hit the ground, his spirit just popped out and rushed at the Israeli soldiers, clawing at them as if he were still alive.

"That's strange," the bishop said. "Doesn't he know he's dead?"

"In one sense, but he's so carnal and devilish already, he wouldn't even recognize the light. He's right where he wants to be."

The bishop looked around and saw that nearly all of his ward members had now made the ultimate sacrifice and were talking with their respective angels.

"Come, it's time to go to the Spirit World," the angel said gently. "Everything is going to be all right."

Over the next several hours, the Megiddo Valley was filled with some of the most violent combat in the history of the world. As the two forces collided, what had begun as a high-tech fight turned into a gruesome hand-to-hand battle as each soldier's bullets ran out during the long day. Millions of soldiers used their rifles as clubs or bayonets as the Battle of Armageddon devolved into a horrible, swarming mass of humanity.

The Israelis fought like lions defending their nation. The battle raged into the evening, but with the numbers stacked so much against them, the Israelis finally started to falter.

Elias urged the Coalition soldiers to finish them off, but as darkness fell it was hard to tell who was the enemy, and exhaustion finally overtook everyone. As if by unspoken agreement, the remaining soldiers on both sides collapsed where they were and slept through the night.

Before the first rays of the morning sun reached the valley, Rachel Cohen opened her eyes. The smell of death immediately reminded her where she was. She had been knocked unconscious during the battle by the swing of a Coalition's soldier rifle. The blow had sent her flying through the air, and she had landed in a crumpled heap. The soldier figured he had killed her and quickly moved on. His haste saved her life.

Rachel could tell sunrise was fast approaching, so she sat up to look around. Through the faint light she could see thousands of bodies surrounding her, and the very ground beneath her was oozing with blood. She had a strong stomach, but the sights and smells were overpowering, and she retched a few times. Finally she stood up and got her bearings.

"Rachel, return to your Uncle Benjamin's home immediately," an audible voice said to her. *"Run before the Coalition soldiers wake up, or you'll be killed."*

She didn't hesitate, sprinting toward Jerusalem through a maze of human carnage. She had to leap over hundreds of bodies that lay in her path, but she knew that voice was absolutely right. If she stopped running, she would die.

CHAPTER 11

———— ✤ ————

Once the sun rose, the battle commenced again and continued for several hours, but eventually the Israeli army was down to only a few hundred soldiers trapped behind a small hill. These remaining soldiers fought valiantly, but they were soon surrounded.

A few of the Israelis begged for their lives, but Elias had made it clear he didn't want any prisoners to worry about. His favorite phrase the past few days had become: "The only good Jew is a dead Jew." His soldiers took him at his word, and these final Israeli soldiers were quickly finished off.

As the battle ended, the Coalition troops systematically worked their way back and forth across the valley, aiding their own wounded but making sure every Israeli truly was dead. If an Israeli had even a faint pulse, he was slain.

The army eventually started moving through the valley toward Jerusalem, but the ground was so covered with bodies from both sides that the lead group had to literally drag thousands of bloodied bodies out of the way to even create a 15-foot wide path for the rest of the soldiers. By late afternoon the surviving Coalition soldiers had gathered on the far end of the Megiddo Valley, completely exhausted.

Elias and General Ramez soon joined them, arriving in their jeeps. The two men climbed up on the hood of Elias' jeep and asked the nearest soldiers to gather around.

"You've all done an excellent job," Elias called out to the soldiers. "Now let's move on to victory. Tonight Jerusalem will be ours!"

The men gave a half-hearted cheer, but it wasn't what they

wanted to hear. They had just endured one of the most gruesome battles in the history of mankind, and they needed to recuperate.

"Uh, shouldn't we set up camp here?" General Ramez whispered to him.

Elias spun on him. "No, it's time to finish this."

The general looked perplexed. "The men are hungry and thirsty. They need a rest. We'd be better off to stay here for now, then move forward tomorrow. The Israelis aren't going anywhere."

Elias' eyes bulged, and he grabbed the general by the throat. "When you have a poisonous snake trapped in a corner, do you step back and let it go, or do you kill it?"

"You kill it," the general wheezed.

"Exactly," Elias said, releasing his grip. "We have two snakes—those apostles—trapped in Jerusalem, and as soon as they find out we've killed all of their soldiers, they'll drop another hurricane on top of us. I know the men are thirsty, but there will be plenty to drink in Jerusalem—including the blood of those apostles!"

In the Israeli military command post, it was becoming clear their nation's army was being destroyed. They hadn't heard from any of their commanders in a couple of hours, and it was possible there weren't any Israeli survivors. A sense of panic set in as everyone realized the Coalition forces would quickly reach Jerusalem.

"We need to check on the women and children at the Jerusalem Center, then we should meet with Benjamin," Josh told Colton. "Let's hurry."

As the apostles left the military building, John the Revelator appeared beside them. "I'll take care of the women and children," he told them. "They'll be safe there. Angels are watching over them. You need to get to Benjamin's house as soon as possible."

Then John vanished, and the apostles broke into a run for Benjamin's home. Josh was knocking on their door within ten minutes, and a pale Benjamin cautiously opened the door. When he saw his visitors, he quickly ushered them inside.

"I'm so glad to see you," he said. "You won't believe who has shown up."

He led them into the front room and pointed at Rachel in the middle of the floor curled in a ball. Her army fatigues were covered in blood.

"What is she doing here?" Colton asked.

"I'm not sure," Benjamin said. "She arrived here less than an hour ago. She was completely worn out and hardly uttered a word before collapsing on the floor. I haven't been able to wake her. I checked her for injuries, and she has a huge bruise on the side of her head. Her pulse is weak, and I'm worried we might lose her. Could you bless her?"

Josh and Colton immediately knelt beside Rachel's head and Josh commanded her in the name of Jesus Christ to be made whole. She stirred, stretched out, then opened her eyes.

"Hello, Rachel," Josh said gently. "Are you okay?"

She looked around the room and then broke down in tears. "Oh, it was horrible," she said, covering her eyes with her hands. "So many dead bodies . . ."

She stood up and hugged Benjamin, who led her to the couch, where he comforted her. After a couple of minutes, Rachel pulled away and said, "I'm going to be all right."

She quickly shared with them the gory details of the previous two days and her belief that none of the other Israeli soldiers had survived the battle. Then she added, "I'd be dead too, except a voice told me to run back here."

"A voice?" Benjamin asked.

"Yes. I believe it was the voice of God. It wasn't my time to die, I guess."

"I don't think it was, either," Josh said. "Remember what we discussed before you went off to battle?"

"Yes," Rachel said. "My uncle and I need to join our remaining people in the Kidron Valley east of the Temple Mount."

"That's correct," Josh said. "The time has come, if you still feel up to it."

"I actually feel really strong right now," she said. "Please let me change out of these clothes, though, and eat something. Then I'll be ready to go."

"That sounds great," Colton said.

"Won't you be coming with us?" Rachel asked. "We could really use your protection."

"No, we need to complete another assignment," Colton said with a tinge of emotion.

"You're welcome to stay here in the house if you need to," Benjamin said. "It's as safe as anywhere."

"Thanks," Josh said, also feeling a bit choked up. "I think we will. That's very kind of you."

The apostles moved toward the Cohens, and the four of them stood with their arms around each other, sensing their lives were about to change forever.

Within fifteen minutes Rachel had showered, changed, and eaten. "We'll see you soon," she told the apostles.

Then the Cohens slipped out the door to gather the remaining Jews to their hiding place near the Mount of Olives.

CHAPTER 12

Within two hours, the first Coalition soldiers entered the gates of Jerusalem. The soldiers were surprised to enter the city without opposition. With none of the inhabitants in sight, the soldiers set dozens of buildings on fire in an effort to scare out anyone who might be hiding inside. A smoky haze soon filled the air as these fires raged out of control.

It wasn't long before the Coalition army occupied half of the city. They did receive some opposition from several guards at the Temple Mount, but those men were quickly killed.

Once the city was clearly under the Coalition's control, Elias entered the city through one of the northern gates. He told his generals, "We must find the two apostles. Nothing else matters right now."

"We haven't seen anyone yet, other than a few guards at the temple," one of the generals said. "The people seem to be hiding from us."

"I can't blame them," Elias said, "but spread the word that I want to meet with the apostles. Shout it in the streets that a great reward will be given to anyone who leads me to them."

Soon hundreds of soldiers filled the streets of Jerusalem, spreading Elias' message. Within thirty minutes the word came back that the apostles had identified themselves to a Coalition soldier and were waiting for him outside a home in Old Jerusalem.

"That was easier than I expected," Elias said upon receiving the news. "But we need to be cautious. It could be a trick."

Elias ordered his jeep driver to follow the directions to the home, and he soon saw several soldiers gathered outside a home he recognized.

"It's no surprise they're at Benjamin Cohen's house," he said to himself. "I should've just dropped a bomb on this place three years ago."

He spotted Josh and Colton standing on the top steps of the home, and a rush of adrenaline filled his veins. They looked so *ordinary*, yet they had thwarted him so many times that he had begun to lose count.

Elias dismounted from the jeep and walked confidently toward the apostles with his arms extended outward as a sign of peace. The apostles didn't move, cautiously watching him as he reached the bottom step and stopped, putting them about 15 feet apart. Thousands of soldiers now filled the street behind Elias, yet the apostles calmly waited for their greatest enemy to speak first.

"I must congratulate you on preserving this city as long as you have," Elias told them. "You are worthy foes. I know you have never had an interest in joining forces with me, but what a team we would have been."

Josh shook his head sadly. "I only feel pity for you, Elias. I remember the potential I saw in you when we first met in Nebraska after one of your speeches. You had a goodness in your eyes that has long vanished."

Elias laughed. "Have I really changed that much? My goal all along has been to achieve world peace, and we are very close to doing that. My methods have simply taken a different direction as opportunities have presented themselves."

"Peace isn't achieved by force and bloodshed," Colton said angrily. "Look at this city! You've killed most of the inhabitants, and your armies are needlessly burning dozens of buildings. Isn't there a better way?"

Elias' eyes narrowed. "How dare you blame me for this! You two are the ones who have caused this destruction. I'm only interested in having Israel join the Coalition, which would have happened long ago without your influence."

"You're wrong," Josh said, "but what do you propose we do? We've been in a standoff for more than three years now."

Elias rubbed his chin thoughtfully. "I hope you can see that the tide has shifted, and my army can't be stopped. However, I want to offer you a goodwill gesture. I'll allow you to fly back to America, rejoin your families, and then talk to your leaders in Zion about how to prepare for another Coalition attack. I think that is only fair, since America is our next target."

Josh didn't believe Elias, but he asked, "You'd really let your two biggest enemies just leave?"

Elias smiled. "Of course. Feel free to discuss it."

The apostles turned toward each other, and in that brief moment Elias pulled a small knife out of his cloak and flung it at Colton, piercing his heart.

"Ohh, he got me good," Colton said as blood seeped through his shirt. He slumped over and then rolled down the stairs into the street.

Josh instinctively hurried down the stairs to help Colton when he felt a sharp pain in his chest as well. Elias' second throw had also hit its mark. Josh staggered forward, made brief eye contact with his attacker, then collapsed in the street within a few feet of where his fellow apostle lay dead.

Elias walked toward them and pulled the knife out of Colton's chest. Then he tried to do the same to Josh, who knocked Elias' hand away as he rolled over onto his back.

"I hope you're proud of yourself," Josh said softly as he pulled the knife from his own chest and tossed it at Elias' feet. "Killing three unarmed men is quite an accomplishment."

Elias stood over him with a smug look on his face. "Why did you say three men?"

"I know you killed my friend Mitko Petrov the same way," Josh said. "He appeared to me after his death and told me what happened. You're pure evil."

A chill went through Elias, knowing Josh spoke the truth. He kicked Josh in the ribs, causing the apostle to groan in agony.

As his strength ebbed away, Josh looked Elias in the eyes and said, "You may have killed us, but you chose the wrong side. Jesus Christ lives! I have seen him, and he will return again very soon."

"That's a lie," Elias said angrily. He abruptly turned and told his guards, "Finish him off."

As Josh endured a brutal beating during the final seconds of his mortal life, he saw Satan standing next to Elias.

"Masterfully done," Satan happily told his earthly leader. "We're completely unstoppable now."

When it was clear both apostles were dead, Elias stepped closer to the bodies once again and shouted, "It is finished! Israel is ours! Let's celebrate this great triumph!"

CHAPTER 13

John the Revelator solemnly watched the apostles' lifeless bodies from a few feet away, unnoticed by the celebrating crowd. His heart was nearly bursting with sorrow at the senseless deaths of his friends. John stayed nearby in case anyone tried to dismember or destroy the bodies, but almost immediately Elias had begun walking toward the Temple Mount and the large crowd followed behind him. Soon the bodies were left undisturbed in the street.

John approached Colton's body first, rolling the apostle onto his back and straightening out his left leg, which had been awkwardly twisted in his tumble down the stairs.

"I just want you to look dignified, my dear friend," John said with emotion.

He also carefully positioned Josh's arms and legs before vanishing from Jerusalem and traveling across the globe in an instant, arriving outside the prophet's home in New Jerusalem just after sunrise there. He knocked gently on the door, and one of the prophet's trusted friends opened it.

"Is the prophet home?" John asked. "I have urgent information to share with him."

The man recognized John from previous visits, and he nodded. "I'll let him know you're here. Come inside."

The prophet soon walked into the room, and John moved forward to give him a gentle embrace.

"I bring terrible news," John told him. "The two apostles have been murdered in Jerusalem by Elias himself. Their bodies are lying in the street, and the Coalition soldiers have taken over the city.

Elias is on his way to the Temple Mount as we speak."

The prophet fought back tears as he said, "We knew this day would come, but the reality of it is still so dreadful. We need to let the Saints know what has happened and declare this a day of mourning throughout Zion."

"I agree," John said. "Just let me know how I can help you."

The prophet paused a moment before saying, "I want you to return to Jerusalem and monitor the situation, but first I would like you to stay while I meet with their widows, Cindy Negus and Kim Brown. I want to break the news to them personally."

"I would like that," John said.

"Thank you," the prophet said. "Make yourself comfortable while I quickly take a shower and change into my suit."

A car was immediately dispatched to bring the women to the prophet's home, and they arrived within half an hour. They were escorted into the prophet's living room, where he introduced John and invited them to sit together on a couch.

"I've been in steady contact with your husbands throughout their assignment, and they have performed spectacularly," John said.

"How are they doing?" Kim asked nervously. "Do you expect them to return home soon?"

The prophet frowned. "Actually, their mission is complete."

John added, "I was in Jerusalem today, where your husbands were killed by Elias of Syria. I'm so sorry."

The women were visibly shaken, and they clutched each other's hands and wept. Both wives had sensed the apostles' mission to Jerusalem might end this way, but the news was still devastating for them.

"What does this mean?" Cindy finally asked.

"This is a key sign that the end is near," the prophet said. "Soon you'll be reunited with Colton."

A sense of peace filled the room, and the prophet and John gave each of the women a priesthood blessing, stating that the Lord was aware of their sacrifices, and that eternal life would be theirs as they endured to the end. Two hours later the prophet addressed the Saints throughout North America via a satellite broadcast, telling them of the recent events in Jerusalem.

"This is a day of mourning, but also a day of rejoicing," the prophet told the Saints. "These beloved apostles are now in Paradise, and their deaths mark a major milestone in the history of the world. Our Savior's return is not far distant."

CHAPTER 14

With his long robe flowing behind him, Elias walked confidently through the temple in Jerusalem and pulled back the veil that led to the sacred room known as the Holy of Holies. Inside the room he saw a golden throne.

"A throne fit for a king," he said with a grin before sitting in the sacred seat. "Get the camera in here! This will be the perfect setting for my broadcast to the world."

Within minutes the camera was in place and the lighting was just right. As the camera began to roll, Elias turned on his charm.

"To the nations of the world, I bring you greetings from inside the Jewish temple in Jerusalem. The Coalition forces have conquered the Israeli people, and I have slain the evil apostles with my own hands. This city is now ours forever!"

The apostles' murders had been videotaped by one of the Coalition soldiers from the roof of a nearby building, and the broadcast quickly switched to an edited copy of the event.

The recording was purposely spliced to delete such things as Josh knocking Elias' hand away and the guards finishing him off, so it appeared that Elias had killed them both instantly with his knife throws.

The broadcast then switched back to a beaming Elias. "With the elimination of our greatest enemies, we now enter the era of peace and happiness that I have long been promising you. Someday you'll tell your children and grandchildren that you were alive when the apostles were slain. This is a day of rejoicing! I declare a three-day holiday throughout the world to commemorate this special occasion. Enjoy yourselves to the fullest!"

The broadcast was shown repeatedly on all television stations, and the news of Josh and Colton's deaths triggered a massive celebration throughout all of the Coalition nations. The citizens poured out into the streets, hugging each other, consuming large quantities of alcohol, and praising Elias' name. The phrase "Gog is great!" was repeatedly chanted by drunken throngs in more than 100 languages.

During his speech, Elias had exaggerated the conquest of Jerusalem, but victory was certainly at hand. Two-thirds of the Jews had been killed, and the Coalition occupied half of the city. Only the Jews who had joined Benjamin and Rachel Cohen in the Kidron Valley had survived.

The Coalition leaders knew where the remaining Jews were hiding, but since they weren't attempting to leave the city, the leaders were content to wait until after the celebration was over to kill them and officially occupy all of Jerusalem.

Despite their tragic deaths, Josh and Colton were feeling very content. In the minutes after their murders, they had watched from above as John tenderly repositioned their bodies. Then to their surprise they had turned to find their beloved Savior standing beside them.

"My dear brothers, you have performed a marvelous work," Jesus said with a warm smile. "Come with me now for a few moments of rest."

The Savior had stepped between them and clasped their shoulders in an embrace as he led them through the veil into Paradise, where they found themselves at the foot of a white staircase. They ascended the steps and passed through a towering golden gate into a natural amphitheater, where a huge throng of Saints had gathered. A loud cheer rang out as the Savior led the apostles to a raised platform surrounded by the Saints.

"This great multitude is preparing to accompany me to earth,"

Jesus said. "They have awaited your arrival as a sign that the moment is nearly here. Take some time to rest and rekindle old friendships, then we'll return to Jerusalem."

The Savior had hardly stopped speaking before Colton was quickly embraced by some deceased friends he had known long ago in England. They all chatted happily, and Colton soon was engulfed by the crowd.

Meanwhile, Josh turned to see his parents, Daniel and Heather Brown, waiting to greet him. He eagerly embraced them both.

"Oh, how I've missed you," he said. "I've thought of you often during the past three years."

"We're so proud of you, son," Heather said. "While you've been away from Kim and the twins, we've been watching over them for you. She's a wonderful mother, and I have to say those children are adorable."

"I can't wait to see them," Josh said.

"Soon enough," Daniel said with a smile. "Follow me to our home. There are more family members there waiting to see you."

As his family members guided him toward their mansion in Paradise, Josh saw a glistening lake that appeared to be made of liquid silver.

"Take a swim in the Living Waters," his father said.

"Really?" Josh asked. "Clothes and all?"

"Go for it," Daniel answered. Josh jumped into the liquid, and it felt like he were floating on air. The liquid somehow extracted from him all of the stress and strife he had experienced while in Jerusalem. Within seconds he felt more rejuvenated and alive than he had during his entire mortal life.

He bobbed to the surface and shouted, "This is fantastic! I feel so much better."

He climbed out of the lake and rejoined his parents. "They really should bottle that stuff," he said.

Heather laughed. "When the Savior spoke of the Living Waters, he wasn't simply using a metaphor. We all take a plunge in the lake once in a while."

The next two days were a wonderfully relaxing time for the two apostles. Seemingly every prophet from Adam on down through the ages wanted to shake their hands and compare "war stories" from their days on earth.

Toward the end of their stay in Paradise, the apostles were led to a magnificent temple to take part in a special meeting where the Savior would outline the final details of his return to Jerusalem.

Seated next to the apostles was a cherished friend from their premortal lives, the Prophet Joseph Smith. They had a few moments to chat before the meeting began.

"I'm excited to go with you during your return to Jerusalem," Joseph told them. "Elias is in for a surprise."

"What do you mean?" Colton asked.

"Hasn't anyone told you yet?" Joseph asked. "As the head of the final dispensation, the Savior has given me the honor of administering the resurrection ordinance to both of you, reuniting your spirits and bodies in celestial glory."

"Won't our enemies know what is going on?" Colton asked.

"No, I'll make sure I'm not visible to any mortals," Joseph said. "It will appear as if you are just waking up from a long nap."

The three of them stopped their conversation as the Savior moved to the front of the room to begin the meeting. They listened intently as he shared details of what awaited them next.

"This is going to be fun," Colton whispered to Josh, who nodded happily.

CHAPTER 15

———— ✿ ————

As the three-day holiday rolled on in Jerusalem, Elias and his Coalition leaders stayed in the temple, hosting an unending victory banquet. The celebration was filled with every manner of wickedness, which completely desecrated and defiled the Lord's house.

"This will make a suitable home, don't you think?" Elias said to his guests, looking around at the temple's gold furnishings. "The Jews have done a marvelous job decorating for me."

On the morning of the third day, the celebration was coming to a close. The people had partied continually without hardly sleeping and were simply worn out.

"Let's go check on the apostles' bodies," Elias said, fighting off a hangover. "Maybe it's time we retrieve them and have them embalmed. Perhaps we can put them on display here in the temple as a constant reminder of what happens when you stand in the Coalition's way."

Soon after the original broadcast of the apostles' murders, Elias had ordered his guards to watch over the bodies at all times. He wasn't going to risk letting the Jews sneak away with them.

As Elias and the other Coalition leaders walked down from the temple and approached the bodies, they expected them to be decaying and covered with flies, but they simply looked asleep, other than some dried blood surrounding the knife wounds in their chests.

"Who moved the bodies?" he shouted at the guards. "I know they were both laying on their sides after I killed them."

The main guard shrugged. "This is how we found them after we came back from the temple that first day. No one has touched them since then."

Elias was feeling irritated as he looked down at Josh's body. "You know what? I never did drink their blood as I had promised. I still would like a little sip to fulfill my oath. Get me some."

The guard looked at him strangely. "Sir, they've been dead for three days. I don't think . . ."

"Just do it!" Elias shouted. "Cut his jugular vein and fill your canteen for me."

The guard hesitantly removed a canteen from his belt, dumped the water out, then pulled out a knife as he knelt down next to Josh's head. He stopped instantly, though, when Josh's eyes opened.

"Aaaaaahhh! Did you see that?" the guard cried, falling back in terror.

"What's wrong?" Elias asked, but then he went speechless as both apostles began to stir. Elias and the other guards gasped and fell to the ground in shock as Josh and Colton stood up. Their spirits had reunited with their bodies, and their wounds were instantly healed. They now possessed celestial resurrected bodies that literally shined with light.

"How are you feeling?" Josh asked Colton, grasping his friend's shoulder.

"Never better," Colton responded.

They nodded their appreciation to a grinning Joseph Smith, who only they could see. Then they glanced at the cowering Elias, but they didn't speak to him because at that moment a voice from heaven was heard saying, "Come up hither."

The apostles looked upward and then pushed off from the ground. They began to elevate rapidly into the air toward a bright light that was descending from the sky.

From her hiding place in the Kidron Valley, Rachel Cohen heard shouts of fear and surprise erupt in the city. She looked upward and saw two people soaring out of Jerusalem and moving quickly toward a small bright light that had appeared several hundred yards above the Mount of Olives.

"What is it?" her uncle Benjamin asked. "A missile?"

Rachel squinted and couldn't quite believe her eyes. "No, there's a man in that light!"

Thousands of people throughout the city watched in awe—including Elias and his soldiers—as the apostles continued to climb into the sky until they reached this glorified being. Then they followed closely behind him as he descended to within a few yards of the mount.

Benjamin put his hand on Rachel's shoulder and cried out, "The Messiah has come! We are saved!"

Just then the Messiah's feet touched the top of the Mount of Olives, and the earth rocked violently as a tremendous earthquake rattled the entire region. Within seconds several hundred buildings in Jerusalem that were occupied by Coalition soldiers tumbled to the ground. Meanwhile, the Mount of Olives split in half, moving apart north to south to create a valley that connected to the Kidron Valley where the Jews were hiding.

The Messiah continued his descent until he came to rest in the new valley. The two apostles joined him there.

Rachel had been knocked onto her back by the earthquake, but she sat up and could see the Messiah in the valley. She felt compelled to lead her people into the valley to greet this powerful visitor, hoping he would protect them from the Coalition soldiers. She hurriedly climbed onto a large rock and shouted, "Follow me! Our Messiah has come!"

The Jews roused themselves from the shock of the earthquake and began to move toward the heavenly beings who were waiting for them. Rachel helped Benjamin along while keeping her eyes on the Messiah. He was standing on a large flat stone so that he was visible to the Jews as they approached him. He was dressed in red—symbolic of the Atonement he had completed during his mortal life when he "trod the winepress" for the sins of all mankind.

"Come closer, my friends," the Messiah told them, and the other Jews looked instinctively toward Rachel, their unofficial spokesperson. She approached the Messiah cautiously and kneeled before him. The rest of the Jews bowed down as well.

"Holy Messiah," she said. "You have finally come."

"Yes, Rachel, I am the Messiah," he said, extending his hand toward her and gently touching her cheek.

Rachel looked at his hand and saw a scar in the palm as if it had been pierced completely through. She noticed that his other hand and feet had similar marks.

She looked into his eyes and asked, "What are these wounds in your hands and in your feet?"

The Messiah said sadly, "These are the wounds with which I was wounded in the house of my friends. I am he who was lifted up. I am Jesus that was crucified. I am the Son of God."

Rachel's heart began to pound and tears came to her eyes as she looked back at the people surrounding her. "Could it be possible?" she asked herself. "Did my ancestors kill their Messiah?"

She swallowed hard and asked him, "Then the events spoken of in the New Testament were real?"

"Yes," Jesus responded. "I lived here in Jerusalem, as recorded by my apostles. I have now returned to save my beloved Jewish people and give them greater knowledge and truth."

"Thank you," Rachel said humbly before looking past him at the two resurrected apostles, who were smiling at her.

"Hello, Rachel," Josh said. "We have risen from the dead, and we are servants of Jesus Christ."

Suddenly the many miracles she had seen them perform came into her mind, as well as the words they had always used: "In the name of Jesus Christ."

"It's all true," she said. She was stunned, but her mind was suddenly enlightened and everything fell into place. She looked back at Jesus. "I want to follow you. Is it possible?"

Jesus smiled kindly again at her. "Yes, my dear Rachel. We will teach you everything you desire."

Then Jesus looked out across the valley and called out, "My brothers and sisters, arise and come forth unto me, that ye may thrust your hands into my side, and also that ye may feel the prints of the nails in my hands and in my feet, that ye may know that I am the God of Israel, and the God of the whole earth, and have been slain for the sins of the world."

The multitude came forward to meet the Lord Jesus Christ, going one by one until they had all gone forth and touched his wounds, from the oldest person to the youngest child. Soon they all knew through their own experience and through the testimony of the Spirit that he was indeed the Messiah—their Messiah.

To their great relief and joy, the King of the Jews had come!

CHAPTER 16

As the Jews met with Jesus, Elias was wandering the streets of Jerusalem in a daze, unsure what to do. The other Coalition leaders stayed close by awaiting orders from him, but Elias was still trying to comprehend how the two apostles had come back to life. He shook his head, not completely convinced it hadn't been a hallucination caused by his three days of drinking.

That didn't explain the light he had seen in the sky, though, or the earthquake that had knocked him to the ground and damaged the buildings around him.

"Maybe that was Satan descending from the sky, coming to steal the limelight from me," Elias said angrily to himself. "Those apostles could have been secretly working for Satan all along, purposely upstaging me all these years."

Elias gritted his teeth, feeling even more confused and angry, when suddenly Satan was standing next to him.

"Run," Satan shouted. "It's your only chance!"

"Was that you in the sky?" Elias asked him.

"No. Just get indoors as fast as you can and hide," Satan commanded before disappearing.

At that moment the heavens seemed to explode above Elias. The sky was filled with fire as a large meteorite entered the atmosphere and shattered into thousands of pieces. Within seconds, chunks of flaming debris showered down on Jerusalem. The newly formed valley was given divine protection from the elements, but all the surrounding area was pelted by baseball-sized molten stones that killed anyone caught in the fiery downpour.

"What's going on?" Elias shrieked. "Satan, where are you?"

A small stone grazed him, catching his cloak on fire. As he spun in horror to put out the flames, he inadvertently stepped into the path of a larger stone, which passed through his chest and completely removed his heart. The stone's heat temporarily cauterized the injury long enough that Elias was still alive as he looked down to see his chest missing.

He took three staggering steps, then fell face first. As he hit the ground, his spirit popped out of his body. He stood nearby as blood began gushing from the hole in his chest. It was gruesome even by his standards.

The molten stones continued to fall, and five seconds later a stone smashed into his head, severing it from his body.

"What a way to go," a familiar voice said next to him. Elias turned to see Satan, who gave him a scolding look. "I told you to get indoors."

"Does this mean I'm dead?" Elias asked.

"Yes, you are," Satan said. "But you should be proud of yourself. You did a masterful job in conquering Jerusalem."

"But how can it end this way? You promised I would rule the world!"

"You did! You were the undisputed leader of the world. Everyone on earth knows your name and face. I just never said how long it would go on. Did you really think it would last forever?"

Elias felt cheated. He wanted to pounce on Satan and beat him to a pulp, but for the first time he saw thousands of dark, hideous creatures standing behind Satan. They were likely human once, but their faces were sinister.

Satan motioned to them and said, "Welcome to the club, Elias! You've earned your spot!"

The demons laughed maniacally, then several of them grabbed Elias, clawing and attacking him as they dragged him away into darkness. Satan waited until Elias' screams of terror faded in the distance, then he fled Jerusalem and headed toward Moscow where he felt more comfortable. He had been only mildly surprised when the two apostles had been resurrected, because it wasn't the first time Jesus had used such tactics. However, he was truly bothered that his enemy had personally come back to Jerusalem and was meeting with the Jews. Whenever Jesus showed himself to the general population it always caused problems.

"I've come too far to let him stop me this time," Satan said angrily to himself as he arrived in the Kremlin. Elias' death would certainly slow his plans for attacking New Jerusalem and the other cities of Zion, but for the most part everything was still on track if they could rebuild the army quickly.

Inside the Kremlin's main hall, dozens of the world's leaders were milling around as if they were puzzled about what to do. They had been reconvening after the three-day holiday when the news came about some possible problems in Jerusalem. Satan listened in on one discussion.

"The scientists say the earthquake surely would've caused many deaths throughout the city," an African leader told a woman. "Then having that meteorite explode above them must have added to the trouble."

"I agree with you, but the top Coalition officials are saying it would be best for us to keep the citizens in the dark about it," the woman said. "They are waiting to hear from Elias before they make any announcements. Most people are barely getting back to work after the holiday and there's no reason to put a scare into them until we have some definite information. Besides, maybe it isn't as bad as we think."

The man shook his head. "Or maybe it's worse than we could have ever imagined."

Satan felt his anger rise, knowing his carefully orchestrated plan to rule Jerusalem had disintegrated. He unleashed a torrent of vile profanity, then began pondering who could be his next earthly leader. It would be a good time to put a military commander in charge, and Elias' best general popped into his mind.

"General Ramez, you're not much to look at, but you'll do nicely," Satan said, picturing the Egyptian's firm demeanor and cold personality. "You've served me so well through the years, but I kept passing you over. Not anymore, though. You're just what I need right now."

CHAPTER 17

—✦—

By the time all of the Jews in the new valley had personally conversed with the Savior, darkness was beginning to fall. The people were basking in a spiritual glow, but they were also quite hungry after such an eventful day.

"Let us go up to the temple," Jesus said. "A meal has been prepared for you."

The crowd parted and allowed him to pass through them, then the True Shepherd led his sheep to the Temple Mount.

Only a small number of the Coalition forces had survived the meteorite storm. Anyone who had been struck by the fiery stones were now dead, and even most of those who had hidden in buildings had not been able to escape the carnage. The stones had crashed through roofs and rolled through the streets, catching many buildings on fire and often trapping and killing the inhabitants. Anyone else among the Coalition forces who had been spared had quickly fled from Jerusalem as the Savior led the Jews out of the new valley.

It was an amazing turn of events. Just that morning the city had been occupied by Elias and the Coalition forces, who had planned to begin killing the remaining Jews that afternoon. Now by nightfall, the Jews were Jerusalem's only remaining inhabitants. After centuries of war and strife, Jerusalem could finally begin to live up to its name as "The City of Peace."

As the Savior and his new flock of followers arrived in the temple's outer courtyard, the people were delighted to see baskets filled with bread and cheese awaiting them, along with beverage containers holding a variety of juices.

Jesus stood quietly in the center of the courtyard and raised his hands. Once everyone was focused on him, he said, "Before we eat, please join me in prayer to our Father in Heaven, who is the source of all our blessings."

He then knelt down to pray, and everyone joined him on their knees as he poured out his heart to his Father, thanking him for numerous blessings and for the meal the Jews were about to consume. The people in the plaza had never heard such a prayer, and the Holy Ghost testified to their hearts once again that this heavenly being was the Son of God.

After the people had eaten, the Savior invited them to rest for the night and then return to the temple in the morning. Josh and Colton had been watching and guiding the people throughout the day, and once everyone began to leave the Temple Mount, the apostles approached the Savior.

"Dear Lord, would it be acceptable if Colton and I visited our families?" Josh asked. "They should just be waking up in New Jerusalem."

"Of course," the Savior said. "I realize you haven't seen them in a long time."

"Thank you so much," Colton said. "Before we go, what other duties do you now have for us?"

The Savior smiled. "I need your assistance here in Jerusalem each day as we fulfill the many promises I have made through the prophets to the Jewish people, but sleep is no longer an issue for you. Please spend your daylight hours here in Jerusalem, and then as darkness falls you can be with your families in New Jerusalem. It will be the best of both worlds for you."

The Savior sent them on their way to see their families, but he asked them to first report to the prophet in New Jerusalem about the day's events before visiting their families. So they dutifully appeared in the prophet's office. They greatly startled him as they materialized near his desk. The prophet let out a shout, then smiled as he recognized his visitors.

"I'm so glad to see you, but next time feel free to arrive outside my office and knock," he said.

Josh shrugged. "Sorry, we're still learning the proper protocol of our new condition."

"I understand," the prophet said with a chuckle. "Just so you know, John the Revelator came here earlier this week with the sad report of your deaths. We visited with each of your wives, and then I announced the news to the Saints."

"How did our wives take it?" Colton asked.

"With a mixture of sadness and relief," the prophet said. "But I explained that it also meant they would see you again soon."

"Yes, the Savior said we could visit our families after we had reported to you."

"Then let's get on with it," the prophet said. "How are things in Jerusalem today?"

"Incredibly better," Colton said. "The Savior has appeared to the Jews, and he led them to the Temple Mount after a shattered meteorite destroyed the Coalition army. Elias is dead, and any remaining enemy soldiers fled for their lives, leaving Jerusalem completely under Jewish control."

"How do you two feel now that your mission is over?" the prophet asked.

"It's a relief to be finished," Josh said. "Once I was in the Spirit World, I realized how much stress we'd been under. I was given the opportunity to swim in the Living Waters, and it recharged me. Of course, being resurrected now takes everything to a higher level."

"I'm very eager for a swim in those waters myself," the prophet said wryly.

The prophet asked a few more questions and arranged with them to join him at the temple that afternoon when he would speak to the Saints again. Then he warmly embraced them.

"Don't spend another minute here," he said. "Your families can't wait to see you!"

The apostles nodded and smiled at each other. Then Colton disappeared to find Cindy and their children, while Josh did the same.

Josh followed the prophet's advice and materialized on his doorstep rather than in the house. He gave a funny knock that he and Kim used to do for each other, then waited anxiously. Within seconds the door flew open and Kim rushed into his arms.

"I just knew you'd come today," she said, kissing him gently then pulling him inside. "The twins are excited to see you. They really only remember you from photos."

As he entered the living room his children Tina and Timothy ran toward him, and he swooped them up. It was an emotional reunion, but Tina made them all laugh when she said, "Daddy, your skin makes me tingle."

Kim quickly explained that Josh was now resurrected, but he was still their daddy and would visit them often. She then turned to him thoughtfully and asked, "By the way, does this mean you're released as an apostle? Will we actually see you more now than we have in the past?"

"No one has said anything," Josh said with a shrug. "I suppose I'm no longer a member of the Quorum of the Twelve, but I'm still an apostle of the Lord. Since I don't need sleep, the arrangement is that I can spend half my day there and half here with you until the Millennium comes. Since Jerusalem is eight hours ahead of you, I'll work there among the Jews until late in the evening, then I'll zip over here to help you with the kids and anything else you need."

Kim smiled. "I'll take that deal."

They moved to the couch to continue talking. While Josh cuddled the kids, he quickly rehearsed to Kim what had happened in Jerusalem during the past few days. When she heard the Savior had appeared in Jerusalem, she asked, "How come we didn't know about it? Wasn't that the Second Coming?"

Josh shook his head. "I suppose the Jews feel it was, but the time for the worldwide Second Coming isn't quite here yet. Don't forget, there is still the final plague to come. It will be worse than all the rest of the plagues combined, but it will be a great day for the Saints, because then Jesus really will come to all the world."

Later that day, the two resurrected apostles stood beside the prophet as he addressed the Saints during a special broadcast from the New Jerusalem Temple's main chapel.

"I have much better news today than I did the last time I spoke to you," the prophet said. "Elder Josh Brown and Colton Negus stand beside me as resurrected beings. I have to say they look better than ever!"

The prophet then invited Colton to share the apostles' recent experiences. The apostle humbly moved behind the microphone and powerfully told of their deaths, their journey to the Spirit World, their resurrections, then joining Christ as he descended to the Mount of Olives. He then mentioned the mixture of grief and joy the Jewish people had felt to finally meet their Messiah, who their ancestors had slain 2,000 years earlier.

Colton concluded by saying, "We are on the cusp of the Savior's return and the beginning of the Millennium. While the rest of the world is unaware of the Savior's coming, you are privileged to know it is very soon—although we still await the dreaded seventh plague. We won't be spared from its effects, but we will fare better than the rest of the world. Needless to say, now is the time to make any final corrections in your lives, so you will be worthy and ready to meet the King of Kings!"

CHAPTER 18

That night, Josh and Colton returned to Jerusalem and were told a meeting had been scheduled to fully organize the Church there. Everyone who had been in the new valley had been converted to the reality of Jesus Christ and the gospel plan, and they wanted to enter the waters of baptism. The mothers and young children who were living in the BYU Jerusalem Center were invited and would be integrated into the new stake.

The big news, however, had been caused by a second earthquake during the night. The quake had triggered a large river of pure water to begin flowing from directly beneath the Temple Mount. This river was several hundred yards wide and flowed eastward through the new valley before turning southward to help heal the Dead Sea.

The Jews had spent the morning swimming and bathing in the river, then dressing in the best clothes they could find in preparation for the upcoming meeting that would be held in the temple's courtyard.

At the appointed time, the Savior appeared and presided over the meeting. After a few words of instruction that were filled with gratitude and love toward the Jews, he introduced several resurrected beings in attendance, including the original Church's First Presidency—Peter, James, and John—and several other Jewish prophets such as Isaiah, Jeremiah, and John the Baptist.

Since their weren't any mortal men in Jerusalem at that time who could confer the priesthood, the same pattern was used as when the priesthood was restored to Joseph Smith. First, John the

Baptist ordained Benjamin Cohen and another man named Joel Frankel to the Aaronic Priesthood, then Peter, James and John ordained the men to the Melchizedek Priesthood. The Savior then invited Benjamin and Joel to walk down the slope to the new river and baptize each other by immersion.

With some coaching from John the Baptist, Joel and Benjamin waded out into the water, where Joel baptized Benjamin, and then they traded places. As the two men waded back to the edge of the river, the thousands of Jews who were watching let out a spontaneous shout of joy.

"I think I know who is getting baptized next," Benjamin said as Rachel leaped into the water toward her uncle. Josh and Colton smiled as two of their favorite people stood in the water together. Benjamin had firmly supported the apostles throughout their assignment in Jerusalem, and Rachel had provided a much appreciated spark among the Jews in those final tense weeks when it was clear the Coalition army was planning to attack the city.

As Rachel walked from the water following her baptism, she moved in the direction of the apostles.

"Thank you for preparing me for this day, even though I didn't exactly understand what you were doing," she said. "But now I see how the gospel all fits together."

"We're so happy for you," Josh said. "We knew you would choose to follow the Savior someday. You've been a great example to everyone."

Thousands of Jews were baptized that day, and the appropriate priesthood office was conferred on every boy and man according to their ages. That evening the Savior announced that there would be one stake organized in Jerusalem, consisting of ten wards. The wards would be created mostly along family lines to simplify making callings and getting the various organizations rolling. There was a great amount of training to do, but that would be taken care of by assigning a few resurrected prophets to each ward to help them get underway.

Benjamin was chatting with Josh and Colton in one of the

temple's outer courtyards when a woman approached them and said to him, "The Messiah would like to speak to you."

Benjamin gave the two apostles a nervous look. "Would you two accompany me?"

"We'd be glad to," Colton replied.

Soon they were standing in the presence of the Savior near the temple, and Benjamin instinctively knelt down. Jesus smiled at the gesture, then motioned for Benjamin to come forward. The Savior put his arm around him and said, "At the suggestion of the two fine men standing with us, I am calling you to serve as the president of the Jerusalem Stake. Are you willing to accept this calling?"

Benjamin looked like he was going to faint, but he nodded weakly. "Yes, I accept."

Josh and Colton came to his side and shook his hand. "You'll do a wonderful job."

Benjamin gave a sigh. "But I don't even know where to begin."

"That's all right," Josh said. "I served as a stake president, and I'll be here to guide you every step of the way."

Benjamin looked greatly relieved. "Thank you. I suddenly feel more confident."

"As the stake president, you're entitled to receive inspiration in selecting your counselors, as well as the presidents of the other organizations," Josh said. "We don't want to twist your arm, but we all feel that your niece Rachel would make a very good stake Relief Society president."

Benjamin's eyes grew wide. "But she's so young!"

"Yes, but she's fully capable, and you'll want someone in that position you can work well with. Besides, all the women already admire and respect her."

Benjamin slowly nodded. "Yes, that's true. I'm already warming up to that idea."

The Savior, the two apostles, and Benjamin then spent some time discussing possible bishops. Benjamin felt understandably intimidated, since the Savior already knew who the bishops would be, but the men let Benjamin discuss each potential bishop, and soon Benjamin felt confident who should be called.

Those ten men were summoned to the temple, and Benjamin issued their callings. Each man was humbled by the calling, but was willing to serve. Rachel was also called to her new position that night, and as she left the temple she sought out the apostles who were waiting outside the room.

She looked Josh in the eye and said, "Do you really think I can handle such a responsibility?"

"Without a doubt," Josh said. "You've already proven to be a great leader."

"Thank you," she said. "I'll do my best."

After Rachel departed, the Savior had one more request for Benjamin. "I know the temple was previously dedicated by a faithful rabbi, but Elias and his followers desecrated the building afterward. I would like you to offer a dedicatory prayer using the Melchizedek Priesthood."

"I would be very grateful for that opportunity," Benjamin said, moving toward the front entrance of the temple. After pausing for a few moments to compose himself, he offered a tender prayer that brought tears to the eyes of the Savior and the apostles.

"I know that prayer came straight from your heart," the Savior said afterward. "I accept this house, which will stand throughout the Millennium."

At the end of the day, Josh and Colton remarked to each other about the miracle that had taken place. An entire stake had been created in a single day—and none of the leaders had been a member of the Church for more than a few hours! But the people were very excited to be a part of the Messiah's kingdom on earth and someday live with him forever.

Several miles to the north, General Ramez could barely put one foot in front of the other. His throat was parched and there was no water in sight. Several hundred Coalition soldiers were with him, but he felt it was a death march. A few drops of rain would have been greatly appreciated, but the sky was clear and the weather was unusually warm, as if Mother Nature intended for them to waste away in the desert.

In retrospect, General Ramez realized he might have been better off to stay in Jerusalem, but after he had seen pieces of the meteorite kill Elias and several of his fellow leaders, he had immediately ran out of the city's north gate with all of the surviving soldiers. They had been on the move ever since.

"Why can't we just admit we're doomed," the general thought to himself, but three days later he and a few thousand soldiers made it to Damascus, Syria. The people gave them food and water, but then sent them on their way toward Russia, fearing an Israeli attack if the soldiers stayed in their city.

General Ramez pushed the troops forward, but unfortunately for them, their immediate future was now out of their hands. Under the direction of the Savior, a 200-mile-wide asteroid had entered the Solar System several months before and had passed near the planet Jupiter. The massive planet's gravity altered the asteroid's course drastically, sending it on a collision course with the third planet from the Sun.

Life on earth would never be the same.

CHAPTER 19

The approaching asteroid was first noticed by Coalition astronomers only a few minutes before it entered the atmosphere over the Atlantic Ocean, a couple hundred miles off the coast of North America. It was thousands of times bigger than the meteorite that had exploded over Jerusalem earlier in the month.

It zoomed westward in the upper atmosphere, triggering immense lightning and firestorms in the sky above North America. The resulting thunder was deafening at times, frightening the citizens of Zion. The asteroid continued to plow through the atmosphere for several seconds before crashing into the Pacific Ocean southeast of Japan and burying itself in the ocean floor near the Mariana Trench, the deepest point on earth.

The effects from the asteroid's impact were dramatic and far-reaching as the impact made the earth actually rock back and forth. The earth's tectonic plates jolted against each other, causing earthquakes along the so-called "Ring of Fire." Within minutes, there was volcanic activity across the globe.

Furthermore, the heat and friction the asteroid had generated in the atmosphere carried westward beyond the point of impact, scorching millions of square miles of forests and destroying cities in eastern Russia and China. Finally, the collision itself had created a monstrous tsunami in the Pacific Ocean that was rushing outward in all directions. The inhabitants of the Hawaiian Islands had been washed away within an hour, as cities along the coast of southern Asia and Indonesia had vanished under the waves. The western coasts of North and South America would be next.

In New Jerusalem, Tad and Emma North had been taking a walk through their neighborhood when the sky seemed to split open and catch fire above them, followed by the loudest thunder they had ever heard. Windows were shattered in homes all along the street, and their neighbors rushed outside.

"What was that?" one man called out.

"I think it was a meteor," Tad called back. "I'm not sure—"

Tad stopped speaking as a deep rumble shook the ground, followed by a sudden shock wave that sent everyone tumbling. Additional jolts came even harder, forcing everyone onto their backs or stomachs.

With great effort, Tad managed to get to his hands and knees. He looked toward the city's center and saw Zion's skyscrapers moving back and forth.

"Wow, that's an unbelievable sight," Tad said. "Emma, look downtown."

"I can't," she cried, unable to even get up on her elbows. She struggled to even raise her head as the shaking continued. "What's happening?"

"Even the temple spire is swaying," Tad said. "This must be the seventh plague. I think we're experiencing the biggest earthquake the world has ever seen."

On the West Coast, Doug and Jonas were outside the Oakland Temple when the meteor zoomed above them, accompanied within seconds by the same powerful earthquake. After the initial shock subsided, they hurried along the hillside to a vantage point where they could see San Francisco. A monstrous crack had formed in a distant shoreline, and they noticed two volcanoes explode several miles to the north.

"Let's pray that we survive," Doug said urgently, clutching his friend's arm.

The men continued to watch in stunned silence as the crack widened to nearly a mile across without a bottom in sight. Portions of San Francisco began falling into the crevice, along with the water from the San Francisco Bay. The rushing water created a huge vortex accompanied by a deafening roar. The special effects in the greatest disaster movies had never come close to matching what they were witnessing.

"Holy Rice-a-Roni," Jonas said in awe as the pyramid-shaped Transamerica Building toppled into the abyss. Despite the magnitude of the moment, Doug couldn't help but smile at Jonas' reference to the food once known as "The San Francisco Treat."

They sat in wonderment for several minutes as the entire area west of them collapsed into the crevice. They breathed a sigh of relief as the crevice finally stopped growing a couple miles away from them, but suddenly they saw a massive wall of water approaching on the horizon. The wave was at least 300 feet high and seemed to grow taller as it got closer to them.

"It's a tsunami!" Doug shouted. "Run uphill or we'll never survive it!"

The two men sprinted up a narrow road, looking backward every few seconds. The waves briefly slowed as the water poured into the large crevice where San Francisco had been deposited, but then the water just kept coming, destroying everything in its path. The waves crashed against Oakland's hillsides, soaking the temple grounds and partway up the building, but then subsiding. Doug looked into the water, which was filled with all kinds of debris from the previous civilization.

Over the next few hours, Jonas and Doug felt like they were stuck on a strange amusement ride, being jolted back and forth by additional earthquakes, while watching the water slowly drain down through the valleys and retreat to the sea. The area where San Francisco had been was now just a huge mud pit. The men eventually walked to the highest point they could find, and they were discouraged when they saw the tsunami had gone inland at least a mile beyond the temple.

Doug finally said, "I think it would be best if we just go back to the temple."

"That's fine with me," Jonas replied. "I'm sure glad we sent that group of Saints to Zion already, because unless we can walk on quicksand, I think we're stuck here for a while."

CHAPTER 20

The meteor's effects had sent Europe and Asia into chaos. Moscow was particularly hit hard by the earthquake, as if the earth itself was tired of the evil ways of the Coalition leaders. The Kremlin complex had folded in on itself, entombing the Coalition delegates inside its walls.

Red Square had a deep chasm right down the middle that was impossible to cross, and the famed circular domes atop the buildings had wobbled wildly before smashing into the streets below. Fires were raging throughout the city, and within hours the remaining citizens had fled. The capital city of the Coalition was now just smoldering ruins.

Throughout Europe and Asia, there was a mass exodus from the cities as the destruction mounted. Families were gripped by fear and hid in caves in the mountains, hoping for some protection from the elements. There was much weeping and wailing among the people, as if the wicked could sense that the end of the world was near and they wanted to hide from God.

Food was the most important commodity anyone could have, but it was difficult to find. The horrible sounds of murder filled the air as the people killed each other over small scraps of meat and bread. Depravity replaced common sense, and any civility quickly vanished. Groups of teenagers roamed the countryside, happily killing anyone who was older than them. They had convinced themselves they would rule the world when the destruction stopped, and they were doing their best to eliminate any competition for power from the previous generations.

✤ ✤ ✤

General Ramez was walking alone along a highway to Moscow when the main earthquake struck. He hid in a small house for a day before starting out again, but he didn't get very far before being approached by a gang of young thugs. Even though he was alone, his intimidating appearance nearly caused the gang to let him pass by, but his army uniform caught their attention.

"Look at his clothes," one hooligan said. "Were you in the Coalition army?"

"I was," Ramez said. "Can you help me? I'm trying to reach Moscow."

"Why do you want to go there?" another boy asked. "The city was destroyed."

"Oh," Ramez replied. "I was hoping it had been spared."

Then without warning several members of the group grabbed the general and pounded his head against the ground, knocking him senseless. Then they stripped him of his clothes and distributed the items among themselves. The one who had grabbed the general's cap tipped it toward him in mock admiration.

"Be careful who you talk to," the boy said with a laugh. "You never know who you might meet."

The group then started walking away as if nothing had happened, leaving Ramez in a pool of his own blood in the middle of the road. An hour later he took his last breath.

In an instant Ramez was standing up and feeling great. For a moment he thought he had miraculously recovered, but then he looked down to see his naked body still on the ground.

"Hello, old friend," a voice said from behind him. The general turned to look at a handsome man with a devilish grin who was surrounded by a group of demons.

"Who are you?" Ramez asked. "Your voice sounds so familiar."

"I suppose it should, "Satan said. "I've been whispering in your ears throughout your adult life. Some call me their master, and I'm the one who led Elias to such great power."

"Elias is dead now," Ramez said. "I saw his body in Jerusalem before I left."

"You're right," Satan said. "That means I have a vacancy at the top of my organization. I think you're the man for the job."

Ramez was silent. There had been many times when he secretly felt he was superior to Elias in every way, but the good-looking one always got the praise. Maybe this was some sort of karma.

"I'd be interested in the job," Ramez said. "But I'm confused. Am I dead?"

Satan waved his hand. "Let's just say you're nearly dead. You'll quickly get back in top form, though."

At that moment Ramez could see a few middle-aged women walking cautiously down the highway toward his body. Satan pointed at them and said, "These compassionate women will take pity on you and nurse you back to health. Once you're recovered, return to Moscow and I'll make sure everything works out better than you could have ever dreamed."

"That sounds good," Ramez said, but he looked past Satan at the hoards of demons and got a bad feeling.

Satan sensed his sudden anxiety. "Don't worry about them. They're on our side—an unseen army that can help solve all of our problems."

Ramez nodded, and suddenly he found himself back in his body. The pain was excruciating and he cried out, which attracted the attention of the women.

"Please help me," Ramez groaned. "I'm a leader in the Coalition army. If you can get me to Moscow, you'll be greatly rewarded."

The women gave him a blanket to cover himself, then they took him to a nearby home, where they fed and clothed him, and took care of his injuries.

Satan watched it all with interest. "Ramez isn't the charmer that Elias was, but he can certainly build another army quickly," he told himself. "I'm back in business."

✤ ✤ ✤

The Saints in Jerusalem were surviving the final plague quite well. The Messiah had departed that first night after organizing the Church, but the resurrected prophets were still there, and they had used their priesthood power to protect the city from further damage.

With the aid of the resurrected prophets, the Jews had returned to the battlefield in the Valley of Megiddo and retrieved the bodies of the fallen Israeli soldiers and buried them at the edge of the battlefield.

The Jews had been prompted to do so by Josh and Colton, who were aware a major prophecy was about to be fulfilled in the areas surrounding Jerusalem. The apostles had shared with the Saints the following scripture in Revelation 19:17-18 and said it would be fulfilled within a week. It read:

And I saw an angel standing in the sun; and he cried with a loud voice, saying to all the fowls that fly in the midst of heaven, Come and gather yourselves together unto the supper of the great God;

That ye may eat the flesh of kings, and the flesh of captains, and the flesh of mighty men, and the flesh of horses, and of them that sit on them, and the flesh of all men, both free and bond, both small and great.

When the Jewish Saints awakened the morning after the final burial, immense flocks of vultures and other birds of prey descended on the battlefield and in Jerusalem itself and began to eat the decaying flesh of the dead Coalition soldiers. The flapping of wings and endless squawking filled the air throughout the day, but by sunset most of the birds had flown away.

The Saints slowly made their way out of their homes, amazed to find only bones remaining where bodies had been before.

"The birds hardly left anything," Rachel told Benjamin that evening as they walked down a street toward the temple. "They picked the bodies clean. I'm disgusted, but I'm impressed."

The frequency of the earthquakes decreased after that horrific day when the asteroid struck, but the volcanoes continued to pump out ash all around the world. The full moon looked like it was covered in blood.

The volcanic ash became so thick that when the sun came up, no sunlight reached the people below. All the earth was shrouded in darkness for two days. Thousands of terrified people in the Coalition nations actually died from fear-induced heart attacks.

The Saints across the world were also frightened by such cataclysmic events, but they also knew that it was always darkest before the dawn. They stayed huddled in their homes with their families, knowing their Savior was watching over them.

On the morning of the third day, the sunlight returned, and the earth was quiet in preparation for a marvelous event that was about to take place. This morning would forever be known as the Morning of the First Resurrection.

At that moment, nearly a million Melchizedek Priesthood holders were assembled in Paradise on a vast green lawn at the base of a massive temple. They were each dressed in their temple robes, ready to return to earth and perform their priesthood duties.

The Savior was teaching them the finer points of the resurrection process and authorizing them to resurrect their family members and friends who were worthy of celestial glory. He also taught them the specific words of the resurrection ordinance that they would perform for each individual.

Each of these men had been given the sealing power during their lifetimes—either as General Authorities or as temple sealers—and during the previous few weeks they had been quietly resurrected from their graves without the world noticing. Many other righteous men were also in attendance who had served as bishops or as the patriarch of a large family. These men had recently been resurrected and given the sealing power as well in order to assist in the great work that needed to be performed.

"Now go forth across the world and seek out your loved ones who have so anxiously awaited this day," Jesus said. "I will inform the angels that the spirits of the righteous may now cross back into the mortal realm and return to their burial locations, where you will meet them and call them forth from their graves."

The men excitedly began vanishing as they journeyed to their respective family burial plots across the world, ready to raise the multitude of Saints that would help erase the stain of evil and darkness from the world.

CHAPTER 21

As the morning sun crept over Maple Mountain after two days of darkness, Mark Dalton felt prompted to go the Springville Evergreen Cemetery. There was a strange silence in the air as he walked through the city. Most of the Saints weren't awake yet, and he enjoyed the solitude.

However, Mark heard voices as he approached the cemetery, and was surprised to see two men dressed in white robes strolling ahead of him. They weaved their way through some headstones before stopping in front of a large older stone.

The men looked majestic and holy, although their faces only looked about 30 and their hair was blond. Suddenly a woman with long brown curly hair appeared next to them. She looked to be in her late 20s and was wearing a red dress. However, she didn't look as solid as the men. She seemed to shimmer, and Mark realized she was a spirit.

One of the men stopped and happily chatted with her, while the other man waved farewell and moved farther into the cemetery. After a few more moments of chatting, the woman put her hand on the headstone and said, "I think I'm ready!"

The man nodded and stated her name before reciting a prayer that reminded Mark of the words used in the LDS temple sealing ceremony. At one portion of the prayer, the woman vanished, but as the man concluded the prayer a few seconds later, she literally emerged from the ground on her back and lay on the grass alongside the headstone.

"So that's how a resurrection is done," Mark said to himself, completely in awe.

Mark noticed there wasn't a speck of dirt on the woman, and the grass was still in place. It dawned on him that she had simply passed through the soil, just like the resurrected prophet Moroni had passed through the ceiling of Joseph Smith's bedroom when he had visited him in 1823.

The resurrected woman was still wearing the same red dress, but now she looked solid and whole. Everything about her was completely amplified in beauty and glory. The man reached down and took her by the hand, and she hopped up from the ground and embraced him.

"Oh, I feel wonderful," she exclaimed. "Let's go find my sister."

The pair then moved down the row to another older headstone. A woman in a blue dress appeared next to them, and the process was repeated as before. Soon she was standing next to them as a resurrected being as well.

Mark realized he had always pictured Resurrection Day as a colossal event when thousands of people would all rise out of their graves at once with the ground opening up and dirt flying everywhere as headstones tipped over.

That scenario had always seemed so messy, so he was delighted to see how orderly it really was. He liked the fact that a resurrection was a personal and individual experience, just like every other priesthood ordinance.

Mark noticed some of the people were being resurrected in their temple clothes, but others weren't. The Spirit whispered to him that the people were being resurrected in the same clothing they were buried in—such as the woman in the red dress. Many men were resurrected wearing army uniforms, although Mark particularly liked the man who came out of the ground wearing a cowboy hat and boots, blue Levis, and a large shiny belt buckle. The man topped it off by giving a triumphant shout of "Yee-haw!"

Mark was amazed at how quickly the numbers of people

multiplied. There were already several hundred resurrected beings in the cemetery within just a few minutes, and Mark realized he needed to check whether anything was happening in the Dalton family plot.

He hurried down the road to the southwest corner of the cemetery where his grandparents Keith and Rosalie Dalton were buried, along with his parents Jack and Sheila, and his grandson Daniel. To his great joy, he saw several Dalton relatives already standing there.

His father Jack saw him approaching and told the others, "Hey, watch out! We've got a mortal among us!"

Everyone turned and happily greeted him. Mark had never met his grandpa Keith during mortality, but they knew each other immediately because they had been close friends in the premortal world.

"You're just in time to watch your grandma come forth," Keith told him. Keith performed the ordinance, and Rosalie quickly emerged through the grass. She modestly smoothed out her white robe and then put a hand to her hair as she sat up.

"Oh, I don't have dirt in my hair, do I?" she asked.

"No, you look fine, dear," Keith said. "You passed right through the soil."

As Keith helped her to her feet, she looked around the group and did a double-take when she saw Mark.

"Hello there, grandson! How's life treating you?"

"It's been a really good day," Mark replied as he gave her a hug. "You look splendid, Grandma. I notice you've gone back to the reddish blonde hair of your youth."

"I think it looks better than white, don't you?" she asked with a smile.

"I do," Mark said, "but it's strange to realize you're my parents and grandparents. You all look fifty years younger than me!"

"You'll look young again soon enough," Rosalie said. "Besides, it doesn't look like I gained any height. I'm still the shortest one!"

After a few more moments of conversation, Jack motioned

toward Daniel's grave, where a particularly handsome spirit in a glowing robe was quietly waiting.

"I figured you'd notice me over here sooner or later," Daniel said with a grin.

Jack turned to Mark and explained, "This would normally be Doug's duty as his father, since Doug holds the sealing power as one of the 144,000 high priests. But since Doug is still mortal, I've been assigned to fill in for him."

Everyone quieted down as Jack called Daniel forth from the grave. Mark was stunned, however, when a pint-sized Daniel emerged from the ground. He appeared to be about four years old, the same age as when he passed away.

"He's so little," Mark said as the miniature Daniel shook out the kinks in his legs and stood up.

"Grandpa Mark, you better watch what you say," Daniel said. "I can talk back now."

Everyone laughed with delight as this boy who had never spoken a full sentence during his mortal life was now bantering with them. Suddenly Daniel surprised them again by leaping into his great-grandma Sheila's arms and hugging her tightly.

"We've become good friends in the Spirit World," Sheila told Mark. "He's such a powerful gospel teacher. I often attended his classes just to listen to him."

They all noticed a woman come running toward them. Daniel wiggled loose from Sheila's arms and ran toward her.

"Mom!" Daniel cried as Becky knelt down and embraced him. They held each other for several seconds, and everyone had tears in their eyes.

Becky finally stood up and said, "A few minutes ago the Spirit told me to hurry to the cemetery. When I saw all the people in white robes, I had a good idea of what was happening. I'm so glad I could be here."

"I had the same impression," Mark said. "I'm sorry I didn't stop to bring you along."

"It's okay. Everything is wonderful," Becky said as she turned to embrace Daniel again before gently caressing his face. "Oh, what a joy it is to see you fully restored. The deformities are all gone."

"Are you and Dad still planning on raising me to adulthood?" Daniel asked. "I promise to be good."

Becky laughed. "Of course. But I have a feeling this might be a case of the child raising the parents."

Across the world, Josh arrived in Moscow outside the collapsed Kremlin complex and made his way to a weed-infested vacant field. Suddenly his friend Mitko Petrov appeared at his side.

"Hello there, old friend," Josh said. "Am I getting close to your burial spot?"

"Yes, it's that sunken area over there," Mitko said, pointing to a barely noticable rectangle of earth.

"I thought that might be it, but I wanted to be sure," Josh said as he walked to the end of Mitko's grave. He performed the ordinance, and Mitko came forth as a resurrected being. He was wearing the clothes he was killed in, but within an instant he switched into a white robe.

"I must say I feel sensational," Mitko said.

"You certainly look sensational, too," Josh said jokingly. "Maybe you might finally find the right girl and settle down."

"That would be nice," Mitko replied.

Josh paused for a moment and surveyed the field. "Is there anyone else here who might be ready?"

Mitko shook his head. "I know there are dozens of people buried here, but they're all here for a reason. They were as wicked as the people who killed them. It will be toward the end of the Millennium before they get resurrected."

"Very well," Josh said, grasping his friend's arm. "Let's get out of here. We have another stop to make."

In an instant they were in the Kaysville City Cemetery in northern Utah, surrounded by many other resurrected beings.

"Who are we here for?" Mitko asked.

Josh didn't answer. Instead, he left Mitko behind for a moment as he walked toward a small headstone where a radiant female spirit was waiting.

"Sorry I'm late," Josh said to his sister-in-law Tina. "Are you ready?"

"Absolutely," she said. Josh recited the words of the resurrection ordinance, and within seconds she rose out of the ground and jumped to her feet. She looked stunning with her dark hair hanging at shoulder length.

Tina had been buried in a nice dress, but she looked down at herself and frowned slightly. "This was my favorite dress when I was a teenager, but now I'm used to wearing something with a little more sparkle."

In an instant Tina changed into a glowing white dress. "That feels more comfortable."

She noticed Mitko standing nearby, so she nudged Josh and asked, "Who is this? Aren't you going to introduce me to your friend?"

"Of course," Josh said, motioning Mitko closer. "I'd like you to meet Mitko Petrov. He's been instrumental in many of the key events in the last days, including giving his life in Russia for the gospel's sake."

Tina smiled warmly at him and extended her hand. "I'm pleased to meet you."

Mitko took her hand, and he quickly discovered that even the heart of a resurrected being can still flutter.

"Yeah, me too," Mitko responded nervously. "Uh, how did you die?"

Josh laughed inwardly at Mitko's awkwardness, but he was secretly pulling for his friend to get his nerves under control. Josh's wife Kim had told him she had a feeling these two might be a good match, which is why Josh had brought Mitko along with him to her resurrection. Maybe that hadn't been the best idea.

"I was hit by a car in Layton, and my body was buried here in Kaysville," Tina said curtly. "Then I went to the Spirit World and accepted the gospel there. My sister Kim performed my temple work, and I've been teaching my ancestors in Spirit Prison since that time."

"That's wonderful," Mitko said, trying to act cool. "I'm sure they're very grateful."

"They are," Tina answered, not quite sure what to say next.

Josh took control of the situation by grabbing each one by the hand and raising them into the air. "We'll have plenty of time to talk later, but the time is growing short," he said. "We don't want to be late."

CHAPTER 22

———— ❧ ————

Josh led Tina and Mitko to a designated location five miles above the middle of the Atlantic Ocean, where they joined millions of other resurrected Saints who had congregated there at the Savior's request. It had been a busy morning getting all worthy people resurrected in time, but at last everyone had arrived.

Josh smiled as everyone mingled with each other. His parents and other ancestors were happily chatting nearby. Mitko spotted some of his friends from Bulgaria and joined them, and Tina had excused herself to visit with her Inca ancestors to whom she had taught the gospel in the Spirit World. Thanks to the temple work her sister Kim had completed in their behalf, these people had been able to be resurrected at this time.

Soon the Lord Jesus Christ appeared, once again wearing his red robe. He was accompanied by his original Twelve Apostles from Jerusalem. The Savior was smiling and seemed quite excited, but he always maintained his magnificent air of dignity and holiness.

"The time has come to banish evil and renew the earth to its paradisiacal glory," the Savior said. "Are we ready?"

"Yes!" the millions of Saints shouted in unison.

"Very good. Please spread out from north to south to encompass the world. Then follow my lead and let yourselves shine!"

Jesus motioned toward an angel standing nearby holding an enormous trump. The angel took a deep breath before playing an amazing musical note that was heard throughout the world.

As the sound echoed throughout the skies, the Savior descended toward the earth and released his full glory as a resurrected being, which was brighter than the sun. Everyone else spread out as the Savior had instructed and also released their full glory, creating a dazzling light effect that stretched for thousands of miles across the sky. The Savior's Second Coming was underway.

The Savior began traveling westward around the earth, with those millions of glorified beings following him, which made it appear as if he were coming from the east. By using a scientific technique similar to that of a huge celestial prism, the Savior made the heavens appear to unroll like a huge scroll, allowing the image of his arrival to be magnified and shown simultaneously to all of the world.

"I am Jesus Christ, of whom the prophets have spoken," he proclaimed for all the world to hear. "I have trodden the winepress alone, and have brought judgment upon all people."

As the Savior soared through the air and approached the America's eastern seaboard, he descended to within a few feet of the ground. The other resurrected beings did likewise, and their combined glory literally burned the earth below them with fire, consuming anything of a worldly and telestial nature. Any item that couldn't abide terrestrial or celestial glory was immediately destroyed.

Emma and Tad North had been preparing breakfast in their home in New Jerusalem when they heard the sound of the heavenly trump. They stepped outside to see what might have caused the sound when an amazing burst of light filled the eastern horizon.

Emma felt herself being lifted high into the air. Her whole body felt tingly and alive, and her skin was glowing. Tad was now at her side, and they clasped hands as dazzling heavenly beings zoomed beneath them, followed by a wall of fire that roared across the earth's surface.

"How are we being protected from the flames?" Emma asked Tad.

"Look at our skin," he said. "We've been transfigured while the earth is being cleansed to usher in the Millennium!"

They saw that the entire population of New Jerusalem had also been lifted up and suspended above the earth. The people called out to each other, sharing their amazement at what was happening. The Saints stayed suspended in the air for a few more minutes until the flames faded away. They slowly returned to earth and noticed a change in their surroundings. New Jerusalem had already been essentially at a terrestrial level, but the Saints now beheld a glorious new world where the most beautiful aspects of the earth had been restored. As the Norths settled back to earth in front of their home, Emma noticed the weeds she had battled in her lawn were now gone, and the grass seemed more lush than before.

The Savior's journey around the world continued over the Cities of Light in the Rocky Mountains, which melted from the fervent heat and became rolling hills. Becky Dalton and her children Heather and Justin had been at Grant School in Springville, and when they were transfigured they actually passed through the roof of the building unharmed.

"That was cool!' Justin said. "I want to do that again!"

As they began moving back toward the ground, they did indeed pass through the roof again and back into the school. The effects of the transfiguration quickly faded, though, as Justin soon found out when he tried to walk through the school's front door and nearly broke his nose.

The Savior and his angelic throng then passed over the coast of California, where Justin's father Doug and Jonas Ferguson had been transfigured and were floating several hundred yards above the earth. Through the flames, Jonas noticed a tsunami approaching from the west that was many times larger than the one they had recently experienced.

"What's that coming behind the wave?" Jonas asked in awe.

"I'm guessing it's another land mass," Doug responded as they watched the waves crash into the coastline beneath them.

"I don't understand, " Jonas said. "How could that be?"

"The continents are moving together again, and during the Millennium there will only be one continent. The Bible says the land was divided during the days of Peleg after the Great Flood, and now the earth is being renewed to the terrestrial state it was when Adam and Eve lived in the Garden of Eden."

"That's incredible," Jonas said as they watched the landscape be transformed by the intense heat. As had happened to the Rocky Mountains, the towering Sierra Nevada mountain range simply melted, and the entire area that was once northern California became a series of gentle valleys and rolling hills.

After a period of time the men settled back to the ground, surrounded by a completely new landscape filled with a variety of beautiful plants and trees, but the Oakland Temple and nearby visitors center still stood. They were the only buildings left in the area.

"I think it's time for us to go home," Doug said. "Let's go see if the truck is still where we left it."

A week earlier, Jonas had suggested they park the truck inside the temple. It seemed peculiar at the time, but now it made perfect sense. They opened a small garage door and found the truck still intact.

"That's a relief," Doug said. "Let's hope this truck can handle some off-road driving!"

"At least it should be a smooth ride," Jonas replied.

CHAPTER 23

In Moscow, General Ramez had heard the trump as well. He angrily went to the window of his office to identify the cause. Instead, he was mesmerized by a brilliant light rapidly approaching from the east. As he raised his arm to block the light, he watched his flesh ignite and begin to turn black.

A wall of flame ripped through the house and torched his clothes. At that point, Ramez's spirit left his body as the flames boiled his blood and burned his body to a crisp. For a few seconds his body stayed upright, but then his charred legs snapped below the knees. Ramez watched in horror as his torso smashed to the ground and shattered into a hundred blackened pieces, while his skull bounced twice before breaking into several shards of bone and scattering his teeth across the floor.

As terrible as that sight was, Ramez was shocked to see two demons suddenly standing near him. They quickly grabbed him and hauled him out of the burning office.

"Where are we going?" Ramez shouted at them.

"We're taking you home," one demon said. "Now that your life is over, Satan wants to remind you where your loyalty lies."

They passed through a veil into Spirit Prison, then they traveled a great distance over desolate terrain to a dark pit at the base of a steep mountain. The demons led Ramez into the pit, which opened up into a monstrous room. Satan was pacing on a ledge at the far end of the cavern.

There were several dozen spirits standing behind Satan, and Ramez recognized them as some of the greatest dictators and terrorists in the history of the world, including Elias of Syria. Meanwhile, there were seemingly millions of restless demons filling the floor of the cave.

Ramez soared down to Elias' side, but his former leader seemed to be in a terrible mood. So Ramez turned to Satan, who he recognized from his near-death experience.

"Can you explain to me what is going on?" Ramez asked. "My body caught on fire, and the whole world seemed to blow up around me."

"We've had a setback," Satan replied. "Our common enemy has brought his resurrected forces to the mortal realm and destroyed everything we have worked so hard to accomplish."

Ramez frowned. "Are you talking about Jesus Christ? I heard his voice—"

"Don't ever say that name!" Satan shouted, his eyes bulging. After a moment, though, he regained his composure. "I assure you this battle is far from over. The people on earth won't listen to us right now, but over time there will be some that will. We may have to wait nearly a thousand years, but those of you who lived as mortals will receive resurrected bodies, and we'll work our way back. Someday we'll rule that world again. We will bide our time and never give up!"

The immense throng in the pit below Satan shouted their support, but then they began to fight and bicker among themselves, eventually devolving into a swarming mass of anger and hatred. Satan glanced at the leaders standing nearby who had devoted themselves to him during their mortal lives. They seemed despondent and unconvinced by his speech, particularly Elias, who stepped forward and motioned with disgust at the other leaders standing on the ledge with him.

"Do you really think this collection of egomaniacs can be organized into anything productive?" Elias asked. "We had our best chance, and we blew it."

"Don't talk that way," Satan told him. "Stick with me, because I know the whole picture. This is all going to work out just as we'd hoped for in the end. You will yet be a great ruler on earth!"

"We'll see," Elias said, shaking his head bitterly. "I don't have any other options now. I see why they call you The Great Deceiver. I feel I got a raw deal."

Before Satan could come up with a response, Elias soared away to a dark corner of the cave to reminisce about the days when he ruled the world.

CHAPTER 24

—⚹—

Meanwhile, the Savior and the resurrected Saints had completely encircled the globe and were coming to a stop above the plaza of New Jerusalem, where the prophet and thousands of Saints had gathered in anticipation of his arrival. He adjusted his level of glory so that the mortal Saints could see him, and the other resurrected Saints did the same, although most of them had now departed to visit their mortal loved ones throughout the world.

Emma and Tad were among the crowd, and they were accompanied by their children David, Charles, and Leah, along with David's wife Phyllis and their young daughter Kiffon.

At that moment the Savior elevated into the air several feet so that everyone could see him. He spread out his arms to the large crowd, and to everyone's surprise, he began to weep.

"Don't be dismayed by my tears, my beloved ones," the Savior said. "These are tears of joy and gratitude for the faithfulness and sacrifices each of you have made for the kingdom throughout your lives. You have built this magnificent city and other Cities of Light, and you have spread the gospel message throughout the world. The long battle against telestial influences is now over, and the millennial era has begun!"

As the Saints gazed upon the Savior, they spontaneously began to sing a song that would forever be known as "The Song of the Lamb." The Saints weren't even sure how they knew the song, but the Spirit was prompting them what to sing. Throughout the plaza the Saints sang out in one voice:

"The Lord hath brought again Zion;
The Lord hath redeemed his people, Israel,
According to the election of grace,
Which was brought to pass by the faith
And covenant of their fathers.

"The Lord hath redeemed his people;
And Satan is bound and time is no longer.
The Lord hath gathered all things in one.
The Lord hath brought down Zion from above.
The Lord hath brought up Zion from beneath.

"The earth hath travailed and brought forth her strength;
And truth is established in her bowels;
And the heavens have smiled upon her;
And she is clothed with the glory of her God;
For he stands in the midst of his people.

"Glory, and honor, and power, and might,
Be ascribed to our God; for he is full of mercy,
Justice, grace and truth, and peace,
Forever and ever, Amen."

As the last words echoed across the plaza, Tad remembered where he had read those words. "I've often wondered how that song would sound," Tad told his family.

"You've heard that song before?" Phyllis asked. "I didn't recognize it, although I somehow sang it!"

"Well, the words are actually in Doctrine and Covenants 84, but I've never heard them set to music. It was more beautiful than I could have imagined."

The Norths slowly worked their way through the crowd to get a better view. Emma and Tad had seen the Savior during the meeting at Adam-ondi-Ahman, but none of their children had seen him in person. As they moved forward, they noticed Kim and Josh Brown standing nearby, along with their twins. Josh spotted them at the same time, and he grabbed Kim's hand and led her through the crowd to the Norths.

"It's so good to see you both," Josh said as he embraced first Emma then Tad. "Wow, look at how these kids have grown! Leah, you're absolutely beautiful."

"Thank you," she said shyly. Her brother Charles nudged her and said, "Wow, it isn't everyday a resurrected being says that about you."

Everyone chuckled, then Tad said, "Josh, we've all followed your activities in Jerusalem, and we're so proud of you. I mean, who would've guessed one of us would end up there? Uh, don't take that the wrong way—"

Josh smiled. "No, I completely understand. I've had some amazing experiences, but I really missed Kim and the kids. I often wished I was still just the secretary of the High Priests group back in Spanish Fork."

As they stood there, the Savior invited any of the mortal Saints who had never met him to come forward. The North children were at the front of the line, and soon they were standing before him.

They were astounded to realize how well he already knew them. He commented to Charles, "You've turned into a master horticulturist! I just knew you could get those pineapples to grow at this latitude."

Then he told David, "I appreciate the work you've accomplished as Elders Quorum president. Your righteous example really touched the hearts of your quorum members."

He then made everyone smile in wonderment by saying, "Leah, Josh Brown is right. You really are beautiful, inside and out. Don't ever let anyone tell you differently."

He then took little Kiffon in his arms. "You will have a wonderful life during the Millennium," he told her.

"I like animals," she suddenly blurted out.

Jesus laughed. "Yes you do, my dear child. You will be a friend and caretaker to many animals throughout your life."

Finally he looked at Phyllis and said, "Thank you for seeking the truth when everything seemed so terrible in Baltimore. You're a wonderful wife and mother, and I'm very proud of you."

Phyllis couldn't contain her emotions as she impulsively embraced him. "Thank you, dear Savior, for everything you've done for me. I can never repay you for the blessings you've brought into my life."

CHAPTER 25

The Norths returned to their homes after visiting the Savior feeling more relaxed and joyful than they had in their entire lives. But within an hour they were in for another big surprise.

Emma shielded her eyes as a bright light moved across the southern sky. The earth jolted a little as the light slipped below the horizon.

"Wow, can you believe another asteroid just hit the earth?" she asked.

"I don't think that was an asteroid," Tad said. "It wasn't moving very fast. Besides, I heard some of the resurrected men discussing the City of Enoch earlier today, and they said we should be expecting it to arrive anytime."

"That's right," Emma exclaimed. "It will be returning to join with New Jerusalem!"

Suddenly Emma felt a little woozy as several premortal memories entered her mind. She slipped to the ground and Tad hurried to her side.

"Are you all right?" he asked.

Emma smiled. "I'm just a little light-headed is all. Remember when I was having those yearnings concerning the City of Enoch? Well, I think I know why. I need to find someone from that city named Susannah who is related to the prophet Enoch. It's strange. I can actually see her face in my mind."

Susannah joined the rest of the citizens of the City of Enoch as they looked into the sky at their beloved earth. The blue-green orb radiated brightly above them, growing larger by the minute. Soon it filled the entire sky, and they could actually see the spot near the center of the continent where their city would fit perfectly. When the earth's tectonic plates had reconnected at the start of the Millennium a few hours earlier, a gigantic hole had remained where the Gulf of Mexico had been—like the last missing puzzle piece. Now the City of Enoch had returned to fill the spot from which it had departed many centuries ago.

Susannah realized that the citizens of New Jerusalem were probably expecting the arrival of a city about the size of Salt Lake City. However, the City of Enoch was really more like a medium-sized nation. During the three centuries it was on the earth, it had expanded several hundred miles in every direction from the main temple and had more than three million inhabitants at the time it was translated.

"The earth is so beautiful," Susannah said to her husband Helam. "I've missed it very much."

Within a few seconds, the city moved close enough to earth that Susannah could see New Jerusalem itself, with the main temple complex clearly visible. Then she felt a sharp jolt as the City of Enoch settled back into its original location.

The people had been told that once the city had returned to earth, many ancient prophets such as Adam. Seth, and Noah would join them and perform a priesthood ordinance to transform each person from their current "translated" level to a resurrected status. Susannah was looking forward to that step up in her eternal progression. Then she would go find her dear friend Emma North.

It wasn't long before the news spread among the Saints that the meteor in the sky was indeed the City of Enoch returning. It had landed directly south of New Jerusalem.

The prophet soon announced to the Saints that he had been notified by Enoch himself that these new arrivals would be coming to New Jerusalem within an hour to meet with the Saints.

"I really need to find Susannah," Emma told Tad. "But where should we go?"

"I think we should stay right here," he said. "Judging from all the premonitions you've been receiving, my guess is she'll come looking for you."

Soon afterward a distinguished couple in shining white robes stood outside the Norths' home. Emma saw them through the kitchen window and immediately rushed outside.

"Emma!" the woman cried out. "It's been too long!"

"I know," Emma responded. "My dear friend Susannah, it's hard to believe I could have ever forgotten you at all."

The two friends embraced, holding each other tightly. Tad came outside and approached the man, extending his hand.

"Hello, I'm Tad. You must be Susannah's husband."

"Yes, I'm Helam."

"It's nice to meet you," Tad said. "Won't you come inside?"

Tad gently tugged at Emma's elbow, and the women wiped their joyful tears and followed the men into the house.

"Pardon the mess," Tad said with a smile. "We had the kids over last night, and the Second Coming kind of threw off our chores this morning."

Susannah laughed and looked around the room. "Emma, your home is beautiful."

"Thank you," Emma said. "We love it here."

"You'll have to come visit our home in the City of Enoch," Helam said. "It actually looks a lot like yours. I suppose I shouldn't be surprised at how similar the architecture is in the two cities."

After a few more moments of small talk, Tad said, "Susannah, Emma has been having brief memories about your premortal friendship, but most of them are a little hazy. Would it be all right if you filled us in on some of the details?"

"Yes, that would be wonderful," Emma said. "It's like I've been reunited with a long-lost sister, but I can't really remember anything we did as kids!"

"I would be happy to do so," Susannah said. "I'll bet you'll be able to remember these things once I start talking about them. The Holy Ghost will open up your mind."

"I look forward to it," Emma said. "Let's get started!"

Emma and Tad sat mesmerized as Susannah talked about how they had become friends almost immediately after being born as spirits, and they had progressed together through all of the spiritual training and preparations for earth life.

Susannah then became emotional and said, "Perhaps this name will spark some memories—Camille."

Emma got a puzzled expression, then she began to sob. Tad turned to Helam and asked, "Are they going to be all right?"

Helam nodded soberly. "Yes, but it's a painful memory."

Finally Emma moaned, "Oh, Camille. How could you?"

Emma then looked at Tad and said, "She was our best friend, and the three of us were inseparable. Camille was beautiful, talented, and excellent in every way, but she had one flaw—vanity. Satan noticed this and he used it against her, promising her that if she sided with him, she could be his queen. We warned her it was all a lie, but she believed him and chose to follow him. It was devastating to us all."

Susannah added, "The rift between us happened gradually at first, but then as the War in Heaven escalated, we each had to make a choice. The four of us all strongly defended Heavenly Father's plan, but to our dismay Camille stood at Satan's side and was cast out with him and the one-third of the spirits that chose not to follow the Savior. We lost many friends that day, but Camille's choice truly broke all of our hearts."

"Where is she now?" Emma asked.

"She obviously didn't become Satan's queen," Susannah said, "but she became an angry, tormented shadow of her former self, promoting wickedness throughout the world."

"It still just makes me sick inside," Emma said. "But she made the choice. We did everything we could to change her mind."

"Well, let's not dwell on Camille," Susannah said. "I'm eager to hear all about your children."

"I'm actually a grandmother," Emma said. "Our little granddaughter Kiffon is a delight."

"A grandma!" Susannah exclaimed with a grin. "Now you're making me feel old."

CHAPTER 26

As the Norths continued their conversation with Susannah and Helam, they noticed the sky outside seemed to be getting substantially brighter. They hurried onto the front lawn and saw that the sky was opening up again like a scroll, as it did during the Second Coming.

An amazing collection of images from world history filled the sky, and everyone across the world was watching the same display. The various scenes showed different events from the earth's history and seemed to be like a celestial screensaver.

"Maybe the Lord is waiting for everyone to get into their seats," Tad said.

Tad's theory seemed correct when after about five minutes a heavenly voice announced they were going to witness a worldwide vision of the history of the world, beginning with the creation of the earth. As the vision started, the images raced across the sky at lightning speed. The panorama was exhilarating yet almost overwhelming.

"This is incredible," Emma said. "Why aren't we experiencing sensory overload?"

"It's like Moses' vision in the Pearl of Great Price," Tad responded. "We can somehow see every person who ever lived and comprehend how everything fits together. It's amazing!"

Within a few moments, the differing theories that had divided religion and science for centuries were quickly put to rest, and everything related to the creation of the earth and the animal kingdom made complete sense.

"Ahh, so that's how the dinosaurs fit in," Tad said.

Next was shown the first of the six 1,000-year periods when mankind had lived on the earth, beginning with Adam and Eve leaving the Garden of Eden and making their way in the world while raising children. Emma was surprised at how handsome and wholesome Cain looked in his younger years, but after he killed his brother Abel he turned into an evil man that led thousands of his descendants into depravity.

"We saw what happened to some of Cain's descendants firsthand," Susannah said. "It was terrible. They became uneducated, living in caves and barely able to support themselves."

"So the cavemen weren't the beginning of mankind, but rather people who had lost the light of the gospel?" Emma asked.

"Exactly," Helam said. "We even sent missionaries to them, but they wanted nothing to do with light and goodness."

The world then saw Adam and Eve raise up another son named Seth, who established a righteous line of descendants. The battle between good and evil continued through the centuries until Adam gathered his posterity in the valley of Adam-ondi-Ahman and blessed them shortly before his death.

"I'm surprised how very little that valley changed in all this time," Tad said, remembering his and Emma's own experience there before the Second Coming.

The second thousand years was highlighted by the City of Enoch being translated. Emma was fascinated to watch Susannah's life right up to the moment the city and all of its inhabitants were taken from the earth.

"You lived such a fulfilling life," Emma told Susannah. "It must have been amazing to watch your city grow and prosper."

"It was wonderful, but I can't wait to see your life," Susannah responded. "I'm guessing your experiences outshined mine."

After the City of Enoch departed, the next major scene was Noah building the Ark and being mocked by the people.

"Once our city left the earth, there weren't many righteous people left," Helam said. "Our remaining relatives who had stayed behind soon passed away, and by the time the Ark was finished, Noah and his family were the only righteous ones still alive. The Lord really had no choice but to cleanse the earth."

The Great Flood was shown in all of its fury, and Tad was astounded. "I had never really envisioned it, but it changed the whole face of the earth," he said.

A memorable scene happened after the Ark had settled onto Mount Ararat and Noah could finally open the Ark's main door to set the animals free. As the door opened, hundreds of mice shot through the opening, scaring the other animals.

Noah's wife gave Noah a stern look and said, "I told you we should've kept those original mice separated!"

Noah simply shrugged, rolled his eyes, and walked away, as if he'd heard that statement a few dozen times in the past few months. The world roared with laughter.

Soon after the Flood, the continents were separated, and the Lord began guiding various families on journeys to repopulate areas throughout the world. Emma really liked watching Egyptus lead her family to the land that would bear her name even before the flood waters had fully receded.

The full story of Abraham, Isaac, and Jacob was well-received, as were the details of Joseph in Egypt and Moses' dealings with the House of Israel for 40 years in the desert. Emma shook her head when some of the Israelites were too stubborn to look up at Moses' brass serpent to be healed after being bitten by snakes. "Sheesh, what a bunch of knuckleheads," she said.

The third thousand years was interesting mostly for the fact that mankind really couldn't get along with each other. The rise and fall of the Jaredite kings in the Americas was shown, as well as the conflicts among the nations in the Eastern Hemisphere. It was disappointing to see the kings of Israel such as David and Solomon throw their eternal blessings away for the things of the world.

"Boy, our American civilization was wicked, but in a lot of ways, they were worse than us," Tad replied.

The fourth thousand years was filled with other interesting journeys, such as when Lehi led his family from Jerusalem to the Americas. It was fun for Emma to see what Nephi and his brothers actually looked like. She whispered to Tad, "Nephi was a strong man, but the paintings the Church once included in the Book of Mormon sure did overestimate the size of his biceps."

Another interesting scene showed the Ten Tribes traveling from Jerusalem to the north countries and establishing their own civilization without any contact with the rest of the world.

As the fifth thousand years began, everyone was enthralled as the Savior's entire mortal life was shown. Even in mortality, he was so much more spiritually advanced—yet more humble—than anyone else. The entire world wept at his betrayal by Judas Iscariot and the ensuing beatings and floggings the Savior endured at the hands of the Roman soldiers.

His agonies in the Garden of Gethsemane and on the cross caused millions of Saints to cry out in a mix of anguish and gratitude for the sacrifice he made to complete the Atonement. Then the mood instantly changed from sorrow to complete joy as Jesus emerged from the Garden Tomb as a resurrected being.

The rapid growth of the ancient Church was enjoyable to see, but as the first century A.D. came to a close, the martyrdoms of the early apostles and the subsequent Great Apostasy left everyone feeling a bit down.

The downfall of the Nephites in the Americas was also hard to watch, but the efforts of Mormon and Moroni were displayed as they preserved the records that would later be translated and published as the Book of Mormon.

The Dark Ages straddled the fifth and sixth thousand years, and it was like watching a dreary well-produced movie that would likely win a bunch of awards, but that left you feeling grimy. The scenes of the Black Plague in particular made a lot of people turn away from watching.

"Tell me when it's over," Emma whispered to Tad.

The scenes started to improve as the sixth thousand years rolled on. A sense of adventure and discovery gripped Europe, and Tad was happy to see Christopher Columbus finally get his due as an inspired explorer who was guided by the Holy Ghost to discover America. He also liked how Martin Luther and other Protestant religious leaders stood for their beliefs and helped usher in the Era of Enlightenment after the publication of the Bible helped the common people learn about God.

The sea voyage of the original Pilgrims was shown, and everyone was riveted by the miraculous founding of the United States against great odds. The hand of God was evident in many ways as George Washington and other patriots held on by the skin of their wooden teeth against Great Britain to create a new nation.

The life of Joseph Smith was shown, and the sacrifices he and other early Saints made to bring about the restoration of the gospel brought tears to Emma's eyes. She had always admired Joseph and Emma Smith, but to see in living color what they actually went through was both inspiring and heartbreaking. The entire world was silent as Joseph and Hyrum were shown being shot to death in the Carthage Jail.

The 1800s and early 1900s zoomed right by, filled with wars and commotion as the restored Church had slow but steady growth. The world seemed to change permanently after the end of World War II as modern inventions made life better but also more spiritually challenging.

The start of the seventh thousand years felt very familiar to Tad and Emma. It was filled with fire and desolation, starting with the attack on the Twin Towers and the war in Iraq, followed by several natural disasters, ranging from Hurricane Katrina to Japan's 8.9 earthquake and tsunami in 2011. Then the political uprisings in the Middle East were shown, along with the severe economic

troubles throughout the world, leading to America's downfall and
the Coalition attack. Millions of people loudly booed when Elias
first appeared, and his rise to power was disturbing to see as Satan
guided his decisions, including the attack on Israel.

Thankfully Colton and Josh had heroically preserved Jerusalem
through the power of the priesthood, and their many amazing
miracles to thwart the Coalition were loudly applauded. There was
a hint of sadness at their deaths, but everyone on earth now knew
how the story ended, and soon the Savior's Second Coming was
replayed in the sky.

As the history of the earth had marched toward its conclusion,
Tad was feeling a bit anxious. He had lived a good life, other than a
few times when he made some mistakes he would prefer the world
not see.

As it eventually reached a segment of Tad's life that he wasn't
proud of, he cringed a little, worried about his sins being shown.
Many shameful acts of millions of unrighteous people had already
been shown, but Tad had faith in the Savior's Atonement, and he
had sincerely repented of his sins and knew he had been forgiven.
Now he just hoped his efforts of repentance had been passed along
to the Grand Editor of this production.

Tad watched intently as his life was shown in the sky, and to
his great relief, certain scenes had been spliced out in some cosmic
editing room. He wept openly at the mercy of the Savior and the
power of the Atonement.

Helam put his hand on Tad's shoulder. "You've lived a great
life, my friend. You can be proud of what you've accomplished to
help the Lord's kingdom roll forward."

Chapter 27

Doug and Jonas had been a few hours into their drive back to Utah when the sky had opened up to show the history of the world. They had stopped the truck and enjoyed the show, and were about to get in the truck and start driving again when a small boy in a white robe appeared next to them, making Jonas jump away in fright.

"Jonas, don't be scared. It's me, Daniel," the boy said with a laugh.

"Why, hello there!" Jonas exclaimed. "You're looking great!"

Doug swept his son off the ground and hugged him tightly. "I was hoping everything had gone well for you today," Doug told him. "Were you one of the angels who zoomed past us at the Second Coming?"

"I was," Daniel said. "Then after we were done, I asked Mom if I could come visit you."

"I'm glad you did," Doug replied. "Why don't you hop in the truck with us and we'll talk as we drive along. I wish we could travel around like you can, but these old mortal bodies still have to go the slow way."

Daniel sat between the two men, and Doug kept looking over at his perfect, resurrected son. "I'm sorry to keep staring at you, but I'm so grateful that you have both arms now."

"That's fine, Dad. Everything has been restored, and I feel great. I think you'll enjoy raising me in this condition."

After a few minutes of discussing what the men had witnessed in San Francisco, Jonas said, "Here's a question I've often wondered,

Daniel. When I was holding you in Manti, were you aware of everything that was going on?"

"Of course," Daniel replied. "I was in constant communication with an angel that night who was guiding me on how to react. He told me when to cry loudly, which is when Dad brought me to you. If I had slept through the night, things would have turned out much differently for all of us."

Jonas started to cry. "Oh, how could I have ever considered doing such a horrible deed? But as you stared into my eyes, I somehow knew you understood I was there to have you all killed. You saved us all."

Daniel patted Jonas on the knee. "It all worked out as it was supposed to. The Lord was watching out for his Saints."

Daniel soon left the truck and returned to Springville to let Becky know the men were returning soon. When they arrived several days later, the Saints held a party in their honor, where they told everyone about their experiences at the Oakland Temple and the destruction of San Francisco.

Doug held Becky close throughout the night and whispered, "I never want to be away from you again."

During the first year of the Millennium, the two world capitals of Jerusalem and New Jerusalem flourished. A modern temple was built near the BYU Jerusalem Center, and temple ordinances were being completed nonstop by the Saints there.

The land of Israel truly became a garden place, and members of the Ten Tribes traveled across the recombined continents to inherit the land in Israel that had been promised to them many centuries earlier.

Peace reigned throughout the land as everyone continued to live the Law of Consecration. Daily life in general was much more simplified, with a major focus on gaining heavenly knowledge, such as learning the details of the organization of the galaxy and universe.

Technology continued to be a part of the Saints' lives. Each home had at least one computer, which was connected to the Church-operated internet system. Families enjoyed watching educational videos or playing religious learning games on their computer. Gospel knowledge that had never been revealed until the Millennium was now easily understood by young children.

The Savior wasn't on the earth at all times, but as the King of Kings he often visited his twin capital cities to consult with his earthly leaders. He had also visited each of the Cities of Light during the past year to allow all Saints to see him personally.

The LDS Church had expanded to have political jurisdiction over all the earth, as well as ecclesiastic jurisdiction over baptized Church members. The main emphasis of the Church during the Millennium was for members to complete the temple work for ancestors who were still in the Spirit World and wanted their ordinances completed. This involved family members on both sides of the veil relaying information back and forth, and it made the entire temple process much more efficient.

There was also a vast missionary effort taking place among the so-called "heathen nations" that had been under Coalition control until the Second Coming. There were millions of "terrestrial" people living there who had survived on the earth and who acknowledged Jesus Christ as the king of the earth, but had yet to join the Church. The conversion rate was astronomical, and great numbers of people were joining the Church each day.

Back in New Jerusalem, Tad had recently been released as the bishop of his ward, and he knew Emma felt a longing to be closer to her family. They continued to live for a brief time in New Jerusalem until one day Tad said, "Hey honey, how about I finally get you a house in Springville, just like you've always wanted?"

She gave him a surprised look. "Do you mean that?"

"I certainly do. I love living in New Jerusalem, but let's move back to be with your parents and Doug and Becky."

Emma gave him a big hug and a kiss. "You've answered my prayers. Let's tell the kids. I think they'll be excited."

Then Emma paused before adding, "I think we need to invite Kim to join us in Springville. Maybe she'll want to stay in New Jerusalem, but I'd love to help her raise those twins."

When Emma stopped by and invited Kim to join them in Springville, she felt like leaping for joy. She had missed being surrounded by friends and family who had known her before she became "Elder Josh Brown's wife."

Not that being Josh's wife was a negative thing. He now spent most of his time completing assignments in the Spirit World and in Jerusalem, but he still always made sure he was home to help tuck the twins into bed.

That evening Kim told him, "Emma and Tad are moving back to Springville, and they asked me if I wanted to join them. I have thought about it, and I really miss their friendship. Becky and Doug are there as well, and I want the kids to know their cousins. So unless you're strongly against it, I'm going to do it."

"I think that's wonderful," Josh said. "I know you'll reconnect with Emma and Becky, and you'll become better friends than ever before."

Kim felt tears welling up in her eyes. "Thank you so much. Staying here in this house just reminds me of all those fearful nights while you were in Israel. It's strange to say when I live in the middle of New Jerusalem, but I'm ready for a change of scenery."

The night before Kim departed for Utah, an attractive couple knocked on the Browns' door. Kim welcomed them into their home, although she wasn't quite sure who they were.

"Don't you remember me? " the man asked. "I'm Mathoni. We knew each other in Guatemala."

"Oh, of course," she said. "Sorry that it took me a moment, but you have to remember I only knew you as an extremely efficient member of the Church, not as one of the Three Nephites.

Don't worry, Josh has since told me about all of your adventures together."

Josh entered the room, and the two men embraced. "I wanted to introduce you to my wife Lamona," Mathoni said.

Josh and Kim shook her hand, and she said, "Kim, I can sympathize with what you're going through of being on separate levels, so to speak. I waited in Paradise while Mathoni completed his earthly mission, and it was challenging at times, but now we're both resurrected and together for eternity."

"I can't wait for that day," Kim said. "Josh and I know this situation will soon pass. We're enjoying watching our twins grow, and at least I don't have to wait 2,000 years like you two did!"

CHAPTER 28

Within a week everyone was living once again in Springville. Mark and Michelle were still living in their home on 100 North where they had raised Emma and Doug. There were a lot of larger homes available, and the Saints would have gladly built them a new home if they wanted one, but they were content to live right where they always had.

"This is where some of our happiest memories happened as you and Emma were growing up," Mark told Doug. "We're completely content to be back where we started so many years ago."

Doug and Becky resumed living in the house next door to his parents, while Emma and Tad moved into a nice home across the street. Kim really liked a home a few doors down, and she and the twins moved in there.

Kim's sister Tina was quite busy in the Spirit World, but she visited Kim occasionally. Their parents were still living in Peru among her mother's relatives, and although Kim stayed in touch with them through video messaging, Tina saw them in person quite regularly.

On one particular morning Tina stopped by to say, "I just saw Mom and Dad, and they are doing great. They told me they want to come visit you soon. They're eager to finally see the twins."

Kim was elated at the news. Josh had also visited her parents a few times since his resurrection, but she hadn't seen them herself since they started their mission in Peru several years before.

"Wow, I can hardly believe it," Kim said with a laugh. "I never imagined when they left on their mission that the Millennium would come before I saw them again."

The twins ran into the room, and the sisters played with them for a few minutes. Then Tina told Kim, "I do want to talk to you about something without little ears listening."

"That can be arranged," Kim said. She corralled the twins and told them, "Hurry across the street and visit Emma. She told me she was making cookies for you."

That's all it took for the kids to scamper out the door.

Tina shook her head. "Ahh, to be five years old again."

They sat in silence for a moment, then Tina asked, "Do you think I'll have to wait until after the Millennium to be sealed to someone?"

Kim had sensed a loneliness in her sister, and she knew the Lord had promised righteous single women like Tina all of the same eternal blessings as everyone else, but Kim wasn't sure about the timing of those blessings.

"I don't think you'll have to wait *that* long," Kim said. "Actually, all the temple sealings need to be completed before the Millennium ends. That's why we're doing temple ordinances around the clock."

"That makes sense," Tina said.

Kim smiled at her. "May I ask if you have someone in mind?"

Tina blushed a little. "Well, I do, but I don't know if he's even interested in me."

"Who is it?" Kim asked, hoping to hear the name of her all-time favorite Bulgarian.

"He was the man who was with Josh when I was resurrected. In the excitement of the moment, I didn't quite catch his name. It was something like Mika or—"

"Mitko," Kim answered happily. "Yes, he's a fine man. One of the best I know, in fact."

"Well, he just acted a little strange that day, so when we were waiting in the sky for the Second Coming to start, I just left to visit my Inca friends and he went off in another direction. Maybe he's already got a girlfriend."

Kim laughed. "With all of his assignments from the Lord, I'm not sure Mitko has ever dated anyone. I would chalk up his unusual behavior to nervousness. Resurrected beings can still get nervous, right?"

"Yes, but how can I be sure how he feels?"

"Well, Josh told me he'd be here this morning. Why don't I have him invite Mitko over right now so you can get to know each other better?"

Tina shrugged, not hiding her interest very well. "I suppose it couldn't hurt."

Josh entered the house a few minutes later, and Kim immediately told him to go find Mitko.

"I'll try, but I'm not even sure he's on earth," Josh said.

"Then you might want to use your connections to locate him. Tina wants to get to know him better."

Josh smiled at that response and gave his wife a kiss. "If that's the reason you need him, I'll search the galaxy for him. I know he wouldn't want to miss this."

Mitko was actually just over in Israel helping the Ten Tribes get settled, and he was knocking on the Browns' door within five minutes. The kids were still over at Emma's house eating cookies, so the four adults sat in the living room and talked about their experiences.

Kim and Josh wisely guided the other two to talk about their common interests, and this time Mitko was much less awkward. He actually apologized to Tina for acting like an idiot at the Kaysville City Cemetery.

"The problem was that when you came out of the ground, I completely lost my train of thought," he said.

"Was I really that ugly?" Tina teased.

"You were hideous," Josh chimed in.

"She was not. She's a gorgeous woman," Mitko said to Josh without thinking. Tina couldn't help but beam as Kim quickly decided to change the subject to Mitko's heroism during World War III.

"Tina, did you know that Mitko basically saved America from the Coalition by himself?" Kim asked.

Tina's eyes opened wide. "No, I didn't."

Mitko shook his head. "She's greatly exaggerating."

"I don't think so," Kim said. "Would the Elders of Israel have defeated the Coalition without you?"

"Um, probably not, but I was just following the promptings from the Lord."

Tina was suddenly seeing Mitko in a new light. "Tell me about it," she said. "What did you do?"

Mitko then humbly told her his life story, and how the Lord had placed him in the Coalition army so he could join the Elders of Israel at the proper time to provide key information and help lead them to victory.

"That is truly amazing," Tina said. "You know what? You could really help me with my current assignment in the Spirit World."

"Yes, you could be just what we're looking for," Kim added.

"What do you mean?" Mitko asked.

"Well, since the Millennium started, I've continued serving in Spirit Prison among my family's ancestors," Tina said. "We've now linked our lineage back from the Incas into actual Book of Mormon times. In fact, the people I'm teaching right now are mentioned in the book itself. I think Archeantus and the people of Sherrizah would love to meet you."

Mitko looked puzzled. "Archeantus and the people of Sherrizah? I've read the Book of Mormon a dozen times and those names don't ring a bell."

"I'm not surprised," Kim said. "I didn't recognize them either until Tina told me she was teaching them. They are mentioned in Moroni 9, the next-to-last chapter in the book. I think everyone just zips past them as they try to finish up."

Tina nodded. "Archeantus was one of the prophet Mormon's great commanders, but he was killed in one of the final battles. Mormon called him one of his 'choice men' who died valiantly. Many of Archeantus' soldiers lived in the city of Sherrizah, and when they were killed in battle, they left behind their wives and children. As the Nephite civilization fell apart around 400 A.D. there were very few priesthood leaders left, so these women and children never had the opportunity to be baptized during their lifetimes. But now they're eager to join the Church, move to Paradise, and soon be resurrected."

"I'm glad you're teaching them, but how could I help?" Mitko asked. "It sounds like you've got it under control."

"We do, except for one group—the husbands who went to war are being a bit stubborn about the gospel. Even after all these centuries, they are holding grudges against the Lamanites and just need to hear the perspective from someone who has been in their shoes. I have tried to teach them, but they just won't listen to me. I really think they would pay attention if the message came from a valiant soldier like you, though."

Mitko was certainly warming up to the idea. "Well, I'm currently helping the Ten Tribes get settled in Israel but—"

"Don't worry about it," Josh said. "I can get your assignment changed without a problem."

"Then let's do it," Mitko said. "I'm looking forward to it."

By that afternoon, Mitko's change of assignment had been cleared, and Tina led him through Spirit Prison to the Nephite city where the people of Sherrizah lived. The people greeted Tina warmly, but they weren't too sure about the newcomer.

Tina gathered everyone around and called out, "This is my friend Mitko Petrov. He lived on earth in the latter-days and was a great warrior in the battle known as World War III. He is greatly respected throughout the mortal realm for his bravery."

"I think you overdid it," Mitko whispered.

"I don't think so," Tina responded. "Look."

Suddenly out of their homes came several men who wanted to see this latter-day warrior.

"Gather around," Mitko said, catching on to Tina's plan. "I want to hear your stories of valor during the final Nephite battles, and I will share my story with you as well."

Mitko was soon sitting in a large room with dozens of Nephite warriors as they began to build friendships. Mitko let each of the men share their war experiences, then he took his turn. The men were fascinated by his description of modern warfare and how even though the Elders of Israel were greatly outnumbered, they had outwitted the Coalition army.

"We were able to do this because we held the priesthood of God," Mitko told them. "Each of you can hold that same power, and then you'll be able to be sealed forever to your precious wives and children. I testify that Jesus Christ lives, and that a wonderful place called Paradise truly exists where you can live with your families. All it takes is a commitment from you. Who has the courage to do as I have done and accept the gospel of Jesus Christ?"

Mitko raised his hand in the air, and slowly but surely every man in the room raised his hand as well.

"Excellent," Mitko said with emotion. "You will never regret the decision you have just made."

At that moment, Mitko noticed the door was slightly open and Tina was watching him. She grinned widely and nodded her approval before shutting the door again.

The response by Sherrizah's men to Mitko's testimony was so overwhelming that other missionaries had to be brought to the city to teach all of the families who were now interested in the gospel. The families progressed rapidly through the lessons, and each day Tina would visit Kim and update her on the names and dates of the Nephites who had accepted the gospel so they could be entered into the Church's family history database.

Then the Springville Saints completed the temple work as soon as possible so the families could move on to Paradise and then be resurrected. It was a busy and exhilarating time for both Tina and Mitko, and they became close friends through the experience.

Two weeks later, Mitko visited Josh and Kim in their home. He said, "As you know, I've been spending a lot of time with Tina in the Spirit World as we teach the people of Sherrizah, and we've gotten along very well. I know this might seem rushed, but I feel Tina is my eternal companion. What should I do now?"

"Ask her if she feels the same way," Josh said.

"Isn't that too straightforward?"

"I think she would actually prefer it that way," Kim said. "If you both feel it is right, do you really feel the need to go through the whole dating and courtship routine? You're already resurrected, after all."

"That's a good idea, but I would feel strange asking her while we were teaching the people. Could you ask her to come over? Maybe I can take her on a walk around the block and see how she feels."

Tina soon arrived, and Mitko invited her to join him on a walk through the neighborhood. Thirty minutes later the couple returned to the house holding hands. As they entered the front room, Tina announced, "We want you to be the first to know that we're going to be sealed for eternity!"

Kim rushed forward and gave them both a hug. "Normally I would say you're rushing into things, but you have both waited so long, and you're such a good fit."

"We wanted Josh to perform the sealing, but it has to be done in our behalf by mortals, right?"

"Yes, but Emma's brother Doug holds the sealing power, and he could do it."

Mitko smiled. "If it is all right with you, Tina, I think we should ask Tad and Emma to be our proxies. Tad was a true mentor to me during our time as soldiers with the Elders of Israel."

"That would make me very happy," Tina said.

"Let's go tell the Norths the good news," Josh said. "I know they'll be very honored."

Tina Marlar looked around the sealing room in the Provo Temple at the curious mixture of mortals and immortals who were in attendance. Her parents had arrived the day before, and she smiled at them. She also gave a little wave to Kim and Josh.

It was an event Tina had hardly dared ponder for herself, but as she stood at the head of the room holding Mitko's hand, she was grateful to have fallen in love with such a valiant soul who had sacrificed his life for the gospel's sake.

"Thank thee, Heavenly Father," she prayed silently. "I have been so blessed."

Mitko was experiencing the same feelings. He and Tina had both died young and unmarried, but the Savior had promised those who lived righteously that they would someday receive all of the blessings of the gospel, and that day had arrived for him. He felt richly rewarded as he turned to gaze at the splendid woman he would spend eternity with.

Doug Dalton stood at their side, and soon he said, "We're ready to begin the sealing ceremony for this special couple, Tina Marlar and Mitko Petrov. They have asked Tad and Emma North to be their proxies, and so I ask Brother and Sister North to now take their places at the altar."

As Tad and Emma knelt across the altar from each other, Mitko and Tina moved closer hand-in-hand so they could watch the proceedings. The ceremony itself took less than two minutes, and afterward both Tina and Mitko immediately acknowledged their acceptance of the ordinance performed in their behalf.

"Then I suppose there is only one thing left to say before we let everyone congratulate you," Doug said with a grin. "Mitko, you may kiss the bride."

TEN YEARS LATER

---✤---

CHAPTER 29

Emma Dalton walked out of the glorious new Springville Temple after completing her morning shift as an ordinance worker.

"I'll see you this afternoon," Emma said to the man at the front desk. "I'm meeting my granddaughter for lunch."

The Springville Temple had been built on Center Street where the Post Office once stood, and there was a beautiful bed of flowers growing along Hobble Creek. That's where her granddaughter Kiffon was waiting.

Every few days Kiffon would meet her there, then they would walk to Emma's home and have an enjoyable lunch together before Emma returned to the temple for her afternoon shift. Emma noticed Kiffon was carefully watching something in her hands.

"What have you got there?" Emma asked.

"A ladybug just landed on me," Kiffon responded. "I'm just studying its spots."

The ladybug flew away, and they smiled at each other. For some reason as the light shone on Kiffon's face, it reminded Emma of her own daughter Leah, who was now married with kids of her own.

"I'm starving," Emma said. "Let's go eat!"

As they walked toward her home, though, Emma's right knee really started to ache. After a few more steps, it developed into a sharp pain down her leg.

"Ouch," she said, coming to a stop. "My leg is really hurting. Can I put my arm over your shoulders?"

Kiffon helped Emma limp the rest of the way home, and then she made lunch for them as Emma sat on the couch and stretched her leg. Although her mortal body had been somewhat rejuvenated during the Millennium, she still battled pains from injuries and surgeries from her pre-Millennial life.

She and Tad—and others in their age bracket—were true relics to these young people as the Millennium rolled on. Kiffon was now 12 years old, and she had no memory of a time when there weren't resurrected beings walking the streets. Emma had recently told Kiffon about how life was before the United States collapsed, and Kiffon had been astonished that people could be so worldly and selfish.

"How did you stay strong with so much temptation around?" Kiffon asked.

"We followed the promptings of the Holy Ghost and the words of the prophet," Emma said. "It took a lot of faith, but we were blessed for keeping the commandments."

In the past ten years, millions of babies had been born to righteous families, and the Lord had decreed that these children would live in mortality until they were 100 years old. They would briefly pass away, then almost instantly become resurrected beings. There was no longer a need for morticians or gravediggers, although the cemeteries were maintained, since there were still millions of souls in the Spirit World who wouldn't be resurrected until later in the Millennium.

As Emma shifted on the couch, her knee throbbed again, but she smiled while remembering what Tad had said a few weeks earlier. He had jokingly said their generation had a "grandfather clause" when it came to living to be 100 years old. Their bodies had been through a lot of stress and strain during the fall of the United States, World War III, and the establishment of Zion, and so most of their generation was dying from natural causes far short of the 100-year mark.

Heart attacks were a fairly common way to go. The Lord had shared with the Saints many ways to use natural herbs to cure cancer and other ailments, but there really wasn't any way to predict a heart attack. Admittedly, no one really minded when it came their time to die, because within a few minutes you were resurrected.

Tad had seemed to sense his time was coming, but his passing two weeks earlier from a heart attack still came as a surprise. Emma had found him dead outside on the lawn, and she called out for help. Within a few moments her resurrected brother Doug had appeared to perform Tad's resurrection.

As Tad rose up from the lawn, he gave Emma a hug before saying with a twinkle in his eyes, "I've just had my life review, and believe it or not, I passed! I have to say, I sure ate a lot of Big Macs when I was younger—and now I wish I'd eaten more!"

Doug's wife Becky had also been resurrected. She had long suffered from the effects of the toxic cloud they'd endured in Spanish Fork Canyon during the Coalition invasion, and one day her body had given out. To everyone's surprise, Doug passed away soon afterward and was quickly resurrected. Emma was still getting used to seeing him with a full head of hair.

Emma had noticed that the Lord was merciful to these older married couples, allowing their deaths to be close together so that one spouse wasn't restored to a youthful resurrected body while the other one stayed in an aging mortal body for too long.

So while it had only been two weeks since Tad's death and he had visited a few times between his new assignments, Emma was definitely looking forward to joining him.

Kiffon brought Emma a sandwich, some baby carrots and a glass of water on a tray. Kiffon quickly finished her meal, but Emma just wasn't feeling well.

"Honey, while I'm finishing up could you go to the temple and tell Brother Hyde at the front desk that I won't be returning for my shift today?" Emma asked Kiffon. "Then come on back and we'll have a nice chat."

After Kiffon left, Emma felt a wave of exhaustion pass over her.

She put the tray on the floor and lay down on the couch, propping up her aching knee with a pillow.

"If I rest a little, maybe it will pass," she told herself.

As she closed her eyes, her spirit left her body, and she saw herself on the sofa. She realized she had passed away, and she said to herself, "There's no way I'm going back. I'm ready to be resurrected."

She felt wonderful as she floated upward toward a bright light. As she entered the light, she saw the Savior beckoning to her in a glorious room. He was seated on a golden throne, but when she arrived he immediately walked toward her.

"Emma, did you know you're one of my favorite people?" he asked, giving her an embrace.

"Thank you," Emma said. "That's good to know, since we're going to review my life, right? I promise to be a bit more serious than Tad apparently was during his life review."

Jesus gave a hearty laugh. "Yes, Tad's review was interesting, but we had a good time. He's a wonderful man. Well, are you ready?"

"I think so."

"You don't have anything to worry about," Jesus said. "These kinds of review are very rewarding for me. Just enjoy it."

A screen flashed on in front of them, and Emma's life was shown from the day of her birth to just a few moments earlier when she had put the pillow under her knee on the sofa. The Savior seemed to be controlling the review, because while everything was indeed shown, including her mistakes, the ones she had repented of were tucked away in the background and barely noticable, as if the Savior was saying to her, "Thy sins have been forgiven. I remember them no more."

Meanwhile, small and simple acts of kindness were brought forward on the screen, and the Savior would comment favorably about the event. He often would pause a scene and show Emma the ripple effect of her kind deeds in the lives of the many people she had affected through her righteous example.

"Though small and simple things are great things brought to

pass," Jesus said. "Let me show you an example of that."

Jesus highlighted a particular day when Emma had followed a prompting to visit her teenage friend Angie, who was struggling as a single mother with her little son Mighty Tom. She was on the verge of making a huge mistake by joining with the false prophet Larry "Sherem" Campbell. That choice would have sent her into a spiritual spiral with major repercussions for not only Angie and Tom, but also many other people throughout the state of Utah. Emma did visit Angie, though, and it forever changed the course of Angie's life for the better.

The Savior also paused the screen on the day Emma found out Tad had received the chip implant.

"Tad and I had a serious talk about this day," the Savior said. "He knew it was wrong and deeply regretted getting the chip, but what he most wanted to talk about was how grateful he was that you had stood by your convictions and not given in to him. You moved to Jolley's Ranch with your parents and children, leaving Tad behind to figure things out for himself. That was courageous and valiant of you, and it was the only way Tad would've ever come to a realization he wasn't living the way he should."

"That was the hardest decision of my lifetime," Emma said as the emotions of that day came back to her. "But I knew if I followed the prophet, things would work out for me in the end, even if it meant I would lose my husband."

The Savior's eyes were misty. "You did the right thing, and by doing so you saved Tad. I'm very proud of you."

They soon finished the life review, and Jesus asked, "What was the highlight of your life?"

Emma pondered his question a moment before saying, "The best thing I ever did was be sealed in the temple to Tad. Even though we had our ups and downs, the last few years of our lives have been wonderful. We've been fully devoted to the Church and raised righteous children."

"Very good," Jesus said. "If I gave you a choice of which kingdom to live in for eternity, which one would it be?"

Emma was a bit surprised by the question, but she said, "As we've seen, I certainly wasn't perfect, and even did some really dumb things, but I have always had faith that the Atonement was real. I've repented of my sins and taken the sacrament each week, and just done the best I could. I do feel I would be comfortable living in the Celestial Kingdom."

"I agree," the Savior said. "Together with Tad, you shall inherit exaltation in the Celestial Kingdom, receiving all that the Father can give you. I have been very pleased with your life, Emma. Thank you so much for all you have done."

The Savior then gave her a gentle embrace, and her mind was opened up to see her premortal life. She had regained a few memories from her chats with Susannah, but she was astonished to see that she had been a great leader there, strongly defending Heavenly Father's plan against Satan's followers. She also saw that just before she departed for her life on earth, the Savior himself had given her a special blessing.

"Because of your faithfulness, all of the promises of that blessing have been fulfilled," Jesus said.

Emma's eyes filled with tears. "You've always been there for me. I'm so grateful."

"And I'm grateful to you for being so valiant despite the many trials you faced. You have been magnificent."

The Savior paused, as if listening to something. Then he said, "Your granddaughter Kiffon has returned to your home and has found your body. She's a little distressed. I'll have Tad meet you there and we'll move forward with your resurrection. We'll meet again soon."

In an instant she was back in her home, watching Kiffon trying to revive her on the sofa. A split second after she arrived, Tad appeared in the room and explained to Kiffon that everything was going to be all right.

"It's time for Grandma to be resurrected," he told her soothingly. "I've been given the sealing power and have been authorized to perform this ordinance, so let's bring Grandma back, okay?"

Kiffon nodded, and as Tad recited the words of the resurrection ordinance, Emma felt herself being pulled back toward her body, When she entered it again, she felt an amazing surge of heavenly energy shoot through her, and she could literally feel her body being changed to a celestial level as every flaw was corrected and restored.

Emma opened her eyes and held her hands out in front of her to see it had transformed into a glorious celestial body.

She stood up and rushed forward to give Tad a big embrace. A rush of love filled her. All of her sadness was gone, replaced by eternal joy.

She also gave Kiffon a hug. "Well, that's not quite how I expected our lunch break to turn out, but I'm happy it did!"

Kiffon soon went to her home to tell her parents about Emma's resurrection, leaving Tad and Emma alone. He took her hand and gave her a long kiss, then he led her in front of a mirror in their bedroom. They laughed with delight at their youthful, attractive faces. They looked to be in their mid-20s, without a single blemish.

"I told you I'd be a great catch someday," Tad said.

"You were always a catch," Emma responded. "I love you so much!"

They embraced, and the happiness and joy that passed between them was more powerful than they had ever felt before. "Wow, I am really loving this new condition," Tad said.

Then he took her by the hand and said, "Why don't we walk down to the temple and let them know they need to find a new ordinance worker to replace you."

"That sounds good," Emma replied. They could have zoomed there instantaneously, but instead they leisurely walked down the street, hand in hand, enjoying each other's company and sharing some playful banter.

"I'm sure glad I stuck with the Tadinator, even when I thought he was going a little crazy," Emma said.

"I'm glad you did too! No one else would have."

Emma smiled to herself. There were other great events awaiting them, such as a reunion with her heavenly parents, and she relished the glorious future she would have with Tad and their family members. Mortality had been challenging at times, but as Emma took another look at her eternal companion, there was no doubt—it had all been worth it.

"Thank thee, Heavenly Father," she prayed. "I am so very grateful to be thy daughter."

Then she slipped her hand from Tad's and playfully sprinted toward the temple, looking back at her surprised husband. She felt so alive and excited about the future that she could hardly contain herself.

"Where are you going?" Tad called out.

Emma laughed and motioned for him to catch up.

"Come on! Eternity is waiting!"

THE END

Bonus Section

If you've read all the way to the end of this series, you clearly have an interest in the last days. As I mentioned in the Author's Note at the front of this book, I would encourage you to read *Through the Window of Life: A Vision of the Glorious Future that Awaits the Lord's Followers* by Suzanne Freeman.

It was after reading Suzanne's experience that I felt prompted to write the *Standing in Holy Places* series, and I simply feel that her inspiring and important message deserves a wider audience. After reading it, you will feel a greater desire to be prepared for upcoming world events and the building of New Jerusalem.

I have received permission from the author and the publisher to include the first chapter of the book here. Thanks again for your support of my series!

Chad Daybell

CHAPTER ONE
Too Busy To Die

Dying is easy. Coming back to life is the hard part.

In 1999, I suffered an ectopic pregnancy and died on a hospital surgery table.

My pregnancy had gone horribly wrong from the moment the embryo attached itself to the inside of my fallopian tube. There wasn't enough room there for a baby to grow, so the tube ruptured and bled, causing me to swell up and take on the proportions of a full term pregnancy in just one day. If it wasn't bad enough that I was too big to tie my own shoes, I also had excruciating pain. To put it in basic terms, my body had turned into one big bruise. Another agonizing element of my condition was that blood enzymes, which travel harmlessly through blood vessels, were irritating my internal organs, triggering a violent reaction from my immune system to fight the "enemy." I could feel every single thrust and parry from the hostile elements battling in my body.

A medical team rushed me to the surgery room in an effort to save my life, but it was too late. Before they hooked me up to any monitors or gave me anesthesia, I died. My spirit floated up against the ceiling. It's a very odd sensation to gaze down at your own body, especially when it's lying on a surgery table, bloated all out of proportion.

I knew that I was dead. I also knew I couldn't stay that way. In spite of the blessed relief from the terrible burning pain of blood

163

filling up my body in places it wasn't meant to be, my spiritual heart was aching. There were seven children at home who needed me.

My husband, a trucker at the time, would never be able to care for all of our children and provide a living for them too. I worried that my children would have to be split up. I couldn't stand the thought of them being sent to different homes, maybe to never see each other again.

So I did the only sensible thing I could think of. I headed back toward my body. No one in the surgery room seemed to notice that I was gone yet, so I figured I could slip back inside with no one the wiser.

But someone above me knew more than I did.

Being so concerned with what I had left behind, I hadn't even thought to glance upward. My single goal was my body lying beneath me, but before I could reach it, I was stopped by a hand encircling my arm.

Startled, I looked down at the hand. It was a man's hand, large and strong, but the most striking thing about it was the puncture wound centered in the back. Before I even raised my eyes to look at the person it belonged to, I knew that I was staring at the hand of Jesus Christ.

Filled with a sudden sense of awe, I looked up to see his blue eyes fixed on me, an expression of delight mixed with intense love emanating from their depths.

Although my heart quickened in the presence of my Savior, I tore my gaze away from him, an unreasoning sense of panic seizing my heart. If Christ had come to get me personally, then my number must surely be up. I still didn't want to go. I couldn't. My children needed me.

I tried to pull away, struggling to break Christ's hold on my arm, anxious to get back to my body before the love and peace I felt from him overwhelmed me and changed my mind. Because I had not been nurtured as a child, I just couldn't bear to leave my children motherless.

Christ put his other hand around my waist to restrain me. With all the love in the world poured into a few simple words, he said, "There are people who want to see you."

"Then you'll have to bring them here, because I'm not going," I said.

I didn't dare glance up at his face again for fear I wouldn't be able to stick to my resolve.

After a moment of silence, a hearty laugh rang out, startling me from my single-minded purpose. Christ was laughing! His laughter was like blending light with love, creating a sound of musical delight. His laughter was also filled with a sense of infinite reassurance that instantly calmed my fears and stopped me from trying to reach my wounded mortal shell.

"I promise I'll bring you back," Christ said, with remnants of his wonderful laughter threaded through his words.

I believed him.

When I looked up at him again, I was surrounded by love so complete that it was like nothing I'd ever felt anywhere on earth. Of course I would go with him. I would follow him anywhere.

I walked beside Christ up a flight of pure white stairs, through a pair of massive golden gates, and into a waiting crowd of my loved ones who had already passed away. There were family members I'd known on earth and others that I hadn't met there, but I recognized them anyway. There was a kind of family connection that resonated in my soul.

We all shared hugs and exclamations of delight at being reunited. Once I'd had a chance to greet everyone, Christ showed me more of this beautiful realm I was in, and my family followed along behind us.

I toured various heavenly cities, and Christ acted as the perfect host while introducing me to several people who had been prominent in earth's history, including the prophet Enoch, Joseph of Egypt, and the founding fathers of the United States of America.

Then Christ led me into a white room, so white that I'm sure it would have hurt my eyes if I'd been in my physical body. It was brighter than the sun beating down on snow at mid-day. It was so entirely white that it was difficult to tell where the wall ended and the floor began. Every surface in the room was of equal brightness, all clean, shining, and glowing white.

Then Christ gestured toward a large screen at one end of the room. Even though the screen was framed by what appeared to be ornate woodwork, the screen's uniform whiteness nearly blended with everything else in the room.

The screen would have been easy to overlook, but once Christ pointed it out to me, it was all I could see. Although there was nothing inherently dangerous about it, I got a cold shiver as I measured its height and breadth with my gaze. It was at least four feet by eight feet. It seemed as though the screen stared back at me with its cold white eye.

I turned to Christ, instinctively putting my back toward the ominous screen. Somehow I knew that it was not there for my peace and comfort.

Christ's eyes softened as he gazed on my apprehensive face. He knew just what I was thinking. He always knows what we're thinking.

"Suzanne," he said in a voice that caressed my name with infinite tenderness. He pointed at the screen. "Through the Window of Life, I can show you some scenes from the last days of the world, things that may happen before I come again."

My heart constricted as I cried out, "I don't want to know!"

I have never been one of those people who are overly interested in what is to come in the future. In high school, I'd read the novel *Fahrenheit 451* by Ray Bradbury. I found it disturbing to read of a future portrayed as a place so bleak and heartless that I was in no hurry to get there.

As for the advent of Christ's Second Coming, I had only read what was in the scriptures. None of the events leading up to his actual appearance sounded very good.

My nerves tight, because I feared his answer, I looked up at the gentle face of Christ. "Do I have to see it?"

Christ pulled me into an embrace that melted every one of my concerns with his loving reassurance. "Of course not."

I breathed a sigh of relief, basking in the unconditional love that surrounded me like a soft, warm quilt. Christ pulled a few inches away and smiled down at me, his eyes gentle and wise, as he said, "But you will save a lot of lives if you do."

The quilt suddenly felt tight, nearly suffocating, and I turned away, instinctively trying to draw in air, even though my spirit didn't need to worry about breathing. I was so new to being dead that I reacted as if I were still in my physical body.

The white screen caught my eye. As I stared at it, it seemed to grow bigger, to loom higher and higher until I felt that it would swallow me whole.

Alarmed, I took a step back and nearly lost my balance. Christ took hold of my arm, his gentle touch warm and reassuring. I glanced down at his hand and again noticed the wound in the back of it, the tortuous wound that had held him up on the cross for hours, his body pulling down against the cruel metal spike that wouldn't let go. He had suffered for me, and now I was cringing at a simple thing he'd asked me to do.

I straightened and turned toward my Savior with a sudden calm resolve. With Christ at my side, I wouldn't be afraid. "Yes, I'll do it."

Christ smiled, a perfect radiant smile that beamed light, brightening the room even more.

"Will you stay with me?" I asked.

Christ encircled me again with his arm as we turned to face the screen. "I'll be with you all the way," he said.

As we watched, side by side, the screen shaded to a pale hue, a light blue that gradually grew in intensity until it became the bright blue of a mid-summer sky. Bits of marshmallow white smudged the edges of the screen, moving inward and converging until they formed clouds that drifted toward me, as stout as sailing ships, as unsubstantial as sea foam. They surrounded me, shifting shape and brushing up against me, sending prickles up and down my arms.

The clouds swirled and parted, closed, opened again, changing my focus until I felt myself flying through the air among them. I was falling.

This wasn't what I had expected, but Christ had never said that I'd be sitting in a padded theater seat with a bucket of popcorn and a soda. I thought I'd be watching a movie like in a movie theater, but now it was clear I would see the things Christ wanted to show me in a more personal way than I had first imagined. Yet, as I fell, I realized that I was unafraid. I could no longer see Christ, but I could feel him beside me, as he promised he would be.

The clouds moved constantly, swirling against my face, then gliding away in a slow ballroom dance. They shifted and parted beneath my feet until I could see the world spread out below, the oceans and continents bright blue and green, alternately shadowed by clouds, then bathed in bright sunlight.

As I flew downward, the world stretched ever farther, from horizon to horizon, until the curve of the earth's surface was lost in the distance. Mountains rose, and rivers sparkled in the sunlight. A small town came into focus.

As I drew closer, I recognized my hometown of Pleasant View. When I was closer still, I saw that I was headed straight for the roof of my own house. Instinctively, I crossed my arms in front of my face and braced for impact.

Through the Window of Life is available through national online bookstores and in several e-book formats.

About the Author

———— ✢ ————

Chad Daybell has worked in the publishing business for the past two decades and has written more than 20 books.

The first four books in this series have all become bestsellers in both the LDS bookstores and the national retail chains.

Chad is also known for his other novels such as *Chasing Paradise* and *The Emma Trilogy*, as well as his non-fiction books for youth, including *The Aaronic Priesthood* and *The Youth of Zion*. He and his wife Tammy also created the *Tiny Talks* series for Primary children.

Learn about Chad and the *Standing in Holy Places* series at his personal website **www.cdaybell.com**.

Chad would also like to connect with you through Facebook. You can reach him at **www.facebook.com/cdaybellbooks**.